---

# A GOOD RESULT

---

## MARG MCALISTER

Blue Gem Publishing

This edition published by Blue Gem Publishing in 2022.

Text and copyright © Marg McAlister 2016



Title: A Good Result | Marg McAlister, author

ISBN: 978-1-922772-98-5 (Paperback edition)

ISBN: 978-0-9924403-8-1 (Ebook edition)



Cover Design by Annie Moril

*V22032022*

# A Little Taste of Paradise

AFTER SETTING up camp with a prime view of the sun-kissed waters of Yamba Bay, Georgie decided that Scott's sisters lived in a place that was pretty close to paradise.

Or so she thought until they went looking for the girls' cafe in the little seaside town, and things suddenly changed. One minute, things were fine; the next, they were not.

Scott's footsteps slowed, and he pointed across the road. "See that window with the coffee cup design? That's their place."

Georgie's gaze followed his finger to the logo of the coffee cup with its curl of steam and the words *Coffee, Cakes, and Crepes,* all in shades of latte and cream and brown.

Her pulse jumped, and a warning shiver ran up her spine.

She glanced at Scott, but he was waiting for a car to pass, and his face showed no concern.

This morning, when they'd left Scott's parents' house, she'd had a sudden feeling that his sisters would need them. Maybe she should have said something to him earlier while they were driving here.

Well, too late now. She would just wait and see what they had to say.

They crossed the road and pushed at the door. It didn't open.

Scott turned the handle and pushed again, but then Georgie, her heart sinking, pointed to the sign dangling from a suction cup on the other side of the glass. *CLOSED.*

"That's odd." Scott frowned. "They're usually open every day in summer."

Georgie put her nose up against the door and peered in. A stack of chairs and tables were just inside the door, ready to be moved outside when the cafe opened for business. The countertops were clear, and the tall glass jars on the counter were empty of cookies.

"Didn't Lissa tell you to call in for coffee as soon as we had set up?"

"That's what she said. But I haven't spoken with her since Wednesday." Scott took out his phone. "I'll see if I can raise her."

Georgie leaned on the door and surveyed the street while she waited for him to make contact, her mind already racing. There were plenty of people strolling along the street and two couples tucking into lunch outside the cafe across the road. From where she stood, she could see four different eateries, all busy.

A glance at her watch showed that it was just before one o'clock; lunchtime. Viv had said their crepes were popular for people wanting a light lunch, so why would they be closed?

Beside her, Scott spoke, keeping his tone light. "Hey! Where are you guys? We're outside your cafe, starving!"

He listened for a moment, and his smile faded. "You're kidding. Okay, then. We'll come to the house, and you can fill us in." He slid the phone back into his pocket and met Georgie's eyes. "Closed down by the authorities."

"*What?*" Of all things, she hadn't expected to hear that. For a moment, she was speechless. "But why?"

"Hygiene concerns. Which is total rubbish; I know my sisters." Scott was already moving, back down the street towards the caravan park. "Lissa's upset."

Georgie hurried along with him, matching his stride. "What did she say?"

"Too long a story for the phone, she said."

Georgie put a hand on his arm but didn't let her footsteps slow. She needed to tell him what was going through her mind.

"Scott. You know this morning when we were leaving, and you said, *I wonder who will need you next?* Or something like that?"

Scott shot her a glance. "You're thinking that it's Viv and Lissa."

She nodded. "Yes—but here's the thing: they came to mind *instantly*."

"Why didn't you say anything?"

"It was just a fleeting thought. And your mother had already mentioned she was concerned about them, so I thought I'd just wait and see what they said when we got here." Georgie jerked a thumb over her shoulder in the direction of the coffee shop. "The moment I set eyes on the cafe…I got this cold feeling. Knew that things weren't right."

"Hmmm." Scott was staring straight ahead, turning things over in his mind. They strode past the gift shop she had browsed a short time before, and headed back to their RV. "Well, whatever it is, we'll be here to help."

2

# A Sad Tale

At his sisters' house, they didn't even have to knock. Lissa opened the front door before they were halfway up the walk.

She gave a twisted smile as her eyes met Scott's. "Hey, bro." Her eyes, precisely the same tawny shade as her brother's, were melancholy, and the dark circles under them signaled a few nights without sleep. Her long straight hair, dyed an adventurous shade of orange, was caught up in a high, messy ponytail.

"Come in and join the wake." Her eyes moved to Georgie. "Not much of a welcome to Yamba for you, Georgie. Sorry about that."

"Don't be silly." Georgie went up to her and hugged her. "Poor you. This sounds awful."

"It is. I don't know how we can come back from this." Lissa moved from Georgie to her brother and submitted to a kiss on the forehead and an affectionate yank on her ponytail. "Ow," she said without heat and gave him an extra hug before stepping back to let them inside.

Her big sister Viv was sitting at the table littered with papers, folders, a calculator, and a wafer-thin laptop in the kitchen. Like Lissa, she looked tired and beaten down. When she saw them, she ran a hand through her short dark hair and attempted a smile. "Scotty, Georgie. Glad you're here." She stood up to hug them both. "So, you're starving, hey? Would a sandwich be okay?"

"I'll make it," Georgie said quickly. "Just tell me where to find everything."

"No, no. Let me." Viv waved a disgusted hand to encompass everything on the table. "I need a break from sitting down and looking at figures, trying to work out what to do."

"Come into the family room." Lissa walked into the small living area adjacent to the kitchen. "We might as well be comfortable while I fill you in."

Georgie and Scott followed her and sat together on a two-seater sofa.

"You start, Lissa," Viv called from the kitchen. "I can listen in from here."

Lissa sat sideways on a chunky armchair and kicked her legs up over the arms. She was wearing white shorts and a loose top, and her tanned legs showed that she didn't spend all her time behind a coffee machine. While they looked at her, she blew out a breath, closed her eyes for a second, and then heaved a huge sigh. "Holy cow, where to start?"

"How about," Scott suggested, "from wherever things started to go wrong? You didn't say anything when you came up to visit a few weeks ago—and when I rang on your birthday, it sounded like everything was fine."

"Back in September." Lissa's voice sounded pensive.

"Yeah, it was. Then in early October, we had a power failure. Lost a freezer full of food, and the electrician turned up a whole bunch of other stuff that had to be fixed to meet code." She made a face. "Expensive."

"But you're leasing," Scott said. "Doesn't the landlord have to fix stuff like that?"

"To a degree," Lisa said. "But in the end, if we want to stay in the same premises—"

"Which we did," Viv called out from the kitchen, "because we were getting regulars as well as the tourists. There was nothing else suitable, and we didn't want to have to start again in some other town."

"Anyway." Lissa waved off that problem and went on. "He made it clear when we took out the lease it was an old building, and he wouldn't be doing too much more work on it. The location was great, so we took it."

"He did offer us another rental," Viv added. "But it wasn't as central, and also an old building. Could have been out of the frying pan into the fire."

"So we stayed," Lissa said. "Next thing: because I run barista courses in nearby towns, we've been using backpackers as casuals. The first girl we had, Svetlana, was fantastic. She moved on after a few months, and the next girl was okay, but then Sean...." She grimaced. "He was a nightmare. Lazy, offhand with customers, and a thief, as it turned out. Our takings were down, and he was the cause."

Georgie was beginning to get the picture. Extra expense for wiring, someone with a hand in the till—not what a fledgling business needed.

"That was at the end of October, so it was a bad month," Lissa said. "But the money from the extra barista job helped keep us afloat."

From the kitchen, Viv's voice floated in. "I'm making tea for myself, coffee for Lissa. What would you guys like?"

Scott raised an eyebrow at his younger sister. "You're letting *Viv* make your coffee?"

Lissa managed a tired smile. "I trained her. Now, it's drinkable."

"In that case," Scott said, "Same for me. Georgie?"

"Yes, same, thanks."

While listening to Lissa, Georgie studied her body language and listened for clues that might tell her what was going on. There was more to come, obviously, and she couldn't shake the feeling that this was more than just a cafe's growing pains. As Lissa spoke, her fingers had been digging into the fabric on the end of the padded armrest, and now she was picking at a loose thread. "I'll wait for Viv to come in before we go on," she said. Her voice was heavy with both weariness and anger.

It seemed pointless to engage in small talk, so the three of them sat there silently until Viv brought in a tray loaded with a plate of sandwiches, a pot of tea, and three cups of coffee.

They all helped themselves to a sandwich and settled in. Lissa shook her head at the offer of food and just locked her hands around her cup of coffee. She took a sip. "Not bad, Vivi. Eight out of ten."

"*Eight?*" Viv narrowed her eyes at her sister threateningly. "I moved past eight weeks ago. You want me to keep making your coffee; I want a better score."

Lissa took another sip. She pretended to consider, staring at the ceiling. "Okay, eight-point-two."

Viv rolled her eyes and poured herself a cup of tea.

"Okay," she said. "I'll take the story from here because the next thing happened while Lissa was running a barista course in Grafton. It was Melbourne Cup day, and I'm rushed off my feet, right?"

Georgie didn't have a clue what Melbourne Cup day was, so she instinctively glanced at Scott. Used to having to interpret, he murmured, "Big horse race in Melbourne, first Tuesday in November. The whole country stops for it."

"I managed to squeeze in a few extra tables," Viv went on, "and I had two backpackers helping out. What happens? I get a phone call from the landlord that people have been complaining they haven't got enough room to walk past on the footpath, and I need to do something about it." She shook her head. "Like how? People are sitting in those seats. What am I supposed to do? Say, 'Excuse me, ma'am, that seat was a mistake, would you mind standing up to finish your meal?'"

"Viv got through by moving one table back inside, which meant that people in there weren't happy because they were crammed in," explained Lissa. "Anyway, we got through the day, but the upshot of that was an official visit and measuring distances and explaining to us what naughty girls we'd been, and we had to reduce the number of tables. By *one third*, would you believe?"

"Just when the peak holiday season was coming up in December," said Viv. "Whoopee."

"Fast forward to late December," Lissa said. "Viv was doing the books and saw that our bills for water usage had gone through the roof. We called in a plumber, and he tracked it down to a cracked water pipe. He sent the bill to the landlord, but we still had to pay for the excess. We could manage it because of the holiday crowd, but it was just more expense."

Georgie and Scott exchanged a quick look. So far, Georgie thought, it sounded like just one bit of bad luck on top of another. But there was something niggling at the back of her mind. Something confirmed by the tense attitude of Scott's two sisters.

Lissa swung her feet back to the floor and sat up straight, staring into her cup of coffee before taking another sip. "I'll adjust that score upwards to an eight-point-five, Viv. I think you're improving."

"It's all the stress," Viv said with a weak attempt at humor. "The quality of the coffee is the only thing I can control."

"It's just not all the things that have gone wrong," Lissa suddenly burst out. "It's the way people are looking at us. The cafe has been closed several times while we fix this and fix that. It's making us look incompetent, as though we don't know what we're doing. And now *this*."

Scott nodded. "Closed down by the authorities? All the other stuff can be put down to pure bad luck and maybe that the building is old. But this? Sounds wrong to me. What's going on?"

There was a long silence while Lissa and Viv looked at each other. Finally, Viv said, "That's what we'd like to know. We're super careful about pests, about cleanliness. You have to be in the food business. Yet suddenly, we've got customers walking out because *cockroaches* are crawling around the floor?"

"And out the back, near the bins, they found rotting food." Lissa's voice was bleak. "I went off at Viv, but she'd been waiting until the place closed to yell at *me*."

Viv put down her cup, sat back in her seat, and folded her arms. "A customer complained about a smell. Now, after an unscheduled visit from a food inspector, we're not looking good."

Georgie was puzzled. "*Was* food going bad?"

"He found the source of the smell," Lissa said. "The inspector. Raw fish… somehow it had slipped down between the kitchen counter and the sink."

"He found more cockroaches too," Viv finished off. "That was it. Cafe closed until we clean things up and prove we're up to code. But raw *fish?*" She and Lissa both looked at Scott expectantly, clearly waiting for his reaction.

"Hmmm." After a beat, he narrowed his eyes. "You don't offer seafood…?"

Lissa bounced to her feet, launched herself across the space between herself and her brother, and flung her arms around his neck. "I knew you'd get it."

Seeing Georgie's puzzlement, Viv smiled at her grimly. "We don't serve fish. Coffee, cakes, and crèpes, but no *seafood* crepes. We don't have any fish on the menu, and we've never cooked any in that kitchen."

Georgie nodded. Now, that feeling of *wrongness* that she'd had was making sense.

*Sabotage.*

3

# The Landlord

"HERE HE COMES." At the cafe, Viv straightened in her chair, her eyes fixed on the man getting out of the car that had just stopped outside. She ran a hand through her short dark hair, casting a nervous look at Lissa.

"Toughen up. He won't bite." Lissa sounded offhand, but Georgie noticed that her eyes, too, were wary.

Georgie didn't expect him to be very sympathetic to their problems, from what the girls had told her about their landlord the day before. Stan Lambert owned half of Yamba and was renowned for putting his interests ahead of his tenants.

The landlord ran up the steps and rapped on the door, then pushed it open and came in without waiting.

"Hi, Stan." Viv stood up and pulled back the fifth chair at the table. "Sit down. Can I get you a cup of coffee?"

"Thanks, but no. I'm due to tee off in about twenty minutes; this is a flying visit." He sat down with them and nodded at Georgie and Scott, clearly wondering what they were doing there.

Viv performed the introductions. "Stan, this is my brother Scott and his partner Georgie…meet my landlord, Stan Lambert."

He nodded and shook hands with both of them. His grip was firm, the handshake perfunctory. Georgie immediately got the unspoken message: his time was valuable, and this meeting was just something he had to get out of the way.

He got straight to the point. "You have *another* problem, I hear. This time it seems to be about pest control and questionable food handling practices…?" He turned in his seat and took a long look around the room. "Looks clean enough now, so I guess you've been busy. Is this going to pass code? Kitchen okay?"

"You've been in here before, Stan, so you know it's *always* clean." Viv's voice was tight, and the flash in her eyes showed that she considered his words insulting.

Stan waved that aside, not even looking at her. "Yes, all right. I'm only concerned with the legalities here. And given previous problems with overload on the wiring and water usage, I'm starting to wonder if you're in over your head. Are you going to be able to continue operating?"

Georgie felt Scott's knee press against hers. She returned the pressure, knowing he was thinking the same thing: if Lambert wanted *Coffee, Cakes & Crêpes* to close so he could use the premises for something else, this string of incidents could be enough to use as leverage to get the girls out.

"All of those things have meant additional expense, that's true," Viv said, managing to keep her voice level.

"And before? I don't know that it was a case of *overloading* the wiring. It seriously needed upgrading. Whether it had been our cafe or someone else's, that still would have been the case."

Lambert narrowed his eyes at her. "I told you when you moved in that I wouldn't be doing any unnecessary work, that it was up to you. The wiring is adequate."

"It is *now*."

Lissa, who had been watching the exchange between her sister and the landlord, stepped in. Like Viv, she was making a heroic effort to stay calm. "That's all water under the bridge. The main thing is, this place is spotless, pest-free, and *successful*. The townspeople like what we offer, and the barista classes are popular. Once the inspection is over, we'll reopen immediately."

He jerked his head in a dismissive nod and then linked his hands together. "I have something to put on the table. I want to see you succeed, so consider this: I now have alternative premises available. Linda Malloy next door is thinking of moving, so this might be a good time for you to relocate as well. The people in the town are used to the two shops being next door to each other, so it could work well if you both move at the same time."

"Alternative premises?" The surprise on Lissa's face showed that this was news to her. She shot a look at Viv. "Where?"

"Over near the mall. Adjacent to the new garden center."

Viv and Lissa both shook their heads simultaneously, but Viv spoke for both of them. "No, that wouldn't work. We need to be here, in the township."

"I'm prepared to give you a deal on the rent: a fifty

percent cut for the first three months. That would help you recoup some of your lost income here." Stan Lambert sat back in his seat and folded his arms, looking confident. In his world, money talked.

"But we get more passing trade here." Viv opened out her hands helplessly. "We need that."

"Once people know where to find you, you'll get plenty of customers."

There was a pregnant silence before Lissa drew herself up and looked Lambert in the eye. "We appreciate the offer, Stan, but we would prefer to stay here. There won't be a problem with that, will there?"

"If you pass the inspection, then no." Lambert smiled, but his eyes were cold. "Of course, I can't guarantee that you'll get the same volume of trade, given the circumstances. People tend to be a bit sensitive about cockroaches in their food."

Instantly outraged, Viv pushed her chair back from the table, looking ready to leap at Lambert. "There was never any question about cockroaches in *food*."

At the same time, Lissa leaned forward and pointed a finger at him. "A customer saw cockroaches on the *floor*. Not in the food. As for how they got there, well, we're a bit puzzled about that. We hadn't seen any cockroaches for months—and we spray for pests *twice* as often as we need to." Breathing hard, she glared at him. "It's almost as though someone *wants* us out of here."

Lambert stared back at her for a long moment and then said in a low, even voice, "That sounds very much like you are accusing someone of engineering your difficulties." He raised his eyebrows. "I trust you're not thinking it's me."

Scott shifted in his chair and straightened up, which had the effect of drawing all eyes to him.

"I'm quite certain that my sisters didn't intend any such thing, Mr. Lambert." His face calm, his voice reasonable, Scott met the other man's eyes. "We can all understand why this situation is upsetting for them. They've put a lot of thought and energy into building up this business—which is, I think, good for the whole town."

Georgie's eyes flicked between Scott and Stan Lambert, and, not for the first time, she admired how Scott was able to defuse a situation with a few words. There was something about his innate calm that seemed to spread to those around him.

Lambert relaxed and nodded. "I do understand that. I think it's worth considering the move, though. The complex I'm talking about is only a few years old, and there is a lot of traffic with a mall nearby." His eyes moved to Viv, acknowledging her as the chief spokesperson. "Go over and take a look, talk about it. I'll keep the offer open for a week. And to make things a little easier for you, and as a show of good faith for what you are bringing to the town, I'll extend the half-rental period to 16 weeks. Can't be fairer than that."

Tightlipped, Viv inclined her head a bare inch. "Thank you. We'll let you know."

Outside the cafe, a car door slammed, and they heard hasty footsteps. The door opened, and an auburn-haired woman dressed in an expensive brand of golfing clothes stuck her head in. "Stan. Come *on*. We're going to be late meeting the others." Completely ignoring the other four, she frowned at her husband.

"Coming, Yvonne. I think we're done here?" He stood up and looked around at them for confirmation.

"Yes." Viv manufactured a reasonably credible smile, but Lissa just nodded, her expression cool.

"Right. Call me about the inspection and to talk more about the new rental." With a nod at Scott and Georgie, he followed his wife back to the car.

"Aaargh!" Lissa banged her head on the table. "I *detest* that man."

Scott put a comforting hand on her shoulder and looked at Viv while he said what they were all thinking. "Well, Viv? Do you think he's the one behind all this? It's pretty obvious he wants you out of here."

Lissa raised her head, her eyes bleak. "I don't know. I honestly don't know."

―――――――――――――――――――

4

## The Vibe

―――――――――――――――――――

Two days later, *Coffee, Cakes, and Crepes* reopened after getting the green light from a council inspector.

Just before the doors were due to open, Georgie finished arranging Viv's newest batch of cupcakes on a tiered stand and stood back to admire them. "Banana rum and apple strudel. Yum. They're too pretty to eat."

"That's why I like making them." Viv filled dusky pink ceramic bowls with paper tubes of lo-cal sweetener, raw sugar, and white sugar and walked around putting one on each table. "It's more like doing craft than cooking."

"Viv's a whiz with cakes and desserts," Lissa said from over behind the coffee machine, tipping fresh beans into the hopper. "I'm the go-to guy for main meals."

"Main meals are boring," said Viv, going back to the kitchen for the salt and pepper grinders. "Although crepes are okay. I don't mind crepes."

"She gets artistic with those, too," Lissa said. "When we first started, Viv was experimenting with clever ways to present them. That soon stopped once we got busy." She grinned at her sister.

Georgie's heart warmed to see the two of them looking more cheerful now they were back in business. After a marathon session with the books, they figured they could coast along for another month while making up lost ground financially.

As long as nothing else went wrong.

Lissa had lost that bruised look under her eyes and was looking sassy in a top and matching shorts in shades of mustard and red ochre. Over that, she wore one of her many aprons; today's reading *I Need Coffee, STAT!* She'd anchored her hair high on her head with a funky clip of some kind, and under the spiky orange fringe, her eyes looked happy.

Then she glanced towards the door, and her lips tightened. "Incoming, Viv," she called, rolling her eyes at Georgie, who was making herself useful by filling napkin holders.

Through the glass door, Georgie saw Scott leave the umbrella he was putting up to open the door for a slim blonde woman dressed in a tight white t-shirt, white knee-length shorts, and blinding white sneakers. She carried a large tray of assorted slices and treated Scott to a wide, flirtatious smile as she edged in sideways, nodding at Georgie and then at Lissa. "Delivery! I'll take these through to the kitchen, shall I?"

Lissa didn't answer.

"Vivi out there, is she?" The woman stopped beside Georgie, watching her stuff more napkins into the holders. "Looks like you girls have got yourselves some help to open up again." She treated Georgie to another high-wattage smile that showed perfect teeth, but her clear blue eyes held no warmth. "I'm Amber. From the bakery."

"Hi. I'm Georgie." Georgie returned her smile, wondering what the history was between Amber and Lissa. She nodded at the tray. "They look nice."

"They are. Shane has won awards for them," Amber said, with a little toss of her head that made her shining blonde hair ripple attractively. "Every cafe in town wants them. Or their customers do." She looked over her shoulder at Lissa. "Don't they, Lissa?"

"Mmf." Lissa clanked around behind the machine, not looking at her.

Amber returned her attention to Georgie. "Cute accent. You're American?"

"That's right. I'm from Indiana."

"How do you know Viv and Lissa?"

"I met their brother over in the States. Now I'm here for an extended vacation."

"Helping to get the cafe back on its feet again?" Amber cast a speculative look from Georgie to Lissa and back again. "Are you staying in Yamba for long?"

There was a rattle of dishes behind the counter, and Lissa stepped out, reaching for the tray. "Here, I'll take that through to Viv."

"No, I've got it." Moving away quickly, Amber walked around the other end of the counter and disappeared through the door to the kitchen, her back view showing her pert bottom to advantage in her trim white shorts. "Hi, Vivi! Your slices are here. Shane has sent his new one to try. I can guarantee it's delicious; I helped him taste-test!"

Lissa put her hands on her hips and glared at the kitchen door. "Never loses an opportunity."

Georgie raised her eyebrows. "What's the problem?"

"To cut a long story short, Viv and Shane Carter at the bakery were becoming an item. Then, a few months ago, along came Amber, the apprentice from hell." Lissa's eyes showed both anger and regret. "You know what a baker's hours are like. In the kitchen, early hours of the morning…they ended up exploring more than new recipes."

"Oh." Georgie felt a pang of sympathy. "So Shane broke it off? How did Viv take it?"

"Not well. She really liked him." Lissa stabbed a finger at the kitchen. "Now *she* likes to rub it in, remind Viv of what she lost."

On top of everything else, Georgie thought. In a small town like this, it'd be tough.

A few minutes later, Amber emerged, swinging the tray from one hand. "Well, I'd better be off. More deliveries to make." She stopped in front of Lissa, and her face assumed a look of cloying sympathy. "I was sorry to hear about all the trouble you've been having. But you can't blame the authorities for cracking down. At the bakery, we're paranoid about hygiene. If customers get sick…."

Lissa's nostrils flared. "There is absolutely nothing wrong with our food handling, storage, hygiene, *anything.* We've always been super careful."

Amber put out a placatory hand. "Oh, I'm sure. I'm not saying you haven't. But *something* went wrong, didn't it? Or you wouldn't have been shut down."

"Amber. Leave it alone." Lissa stared her down. "If you don't mind, we're a bit busy."

"Now I've upset you," Amber said, pretending

regret. "I didn't mean to do that. Everyone I've talked to about it, they all say—"

"Maybe it would be a good idea if you *stopped* talking about it," snapped Lissa. She turned her back and stalked back behind the counter.

"Of course." Amber held out slim fingers to Georgie. "It was nice meeting you. I hope you can help get the place back on its feet."

Georgie took her hand as briefly as she could while still being polite. Amber's hand, she reflected, was as cold as her heart.

Amber let herself out, and Georgie watched while she took a moment to flirt with Scott, perching on the edge of one table and lifting a hand to sweep back her rippling honey-colored hair. It was easy to see how a baker could be tempted in the quiet, dark hours of the early morning.

Maybe it was a good thing Viv had found out what Shane was like before she got too involved.

As though summoned by her thoughts, Viv emerged from the kitchen with two small trays of slices to add to the display cabinet. Her eyes found Lissa's immediately, and she grimaced.

"I keep telling you," Lissa said, "you should arrange an accident. Involving, say, a carving knife."

"Lucky we don't have any, then." Viv put the cakes in the cabinet and checked the time. "Five minutes to opening."

"And here's our first customer. Early as always." Lissa nodded at the door, where a tradesman wearing hi-vis clothing was calling out a cheery greeting to Scott as he pushed his way through the door.

"G'day, love." He marched up to the counter. "The

usual. Try not to close again, will you? That pig swill they serve across the street doesn't do the job." He glanced at the kitchen, raised his voice, and called, "Hey Vivi! Good to see you back!"

She popped her head around the door and waved. "Good to be here. Take one of today's cupcakes with you. Present for our favorite tradie."

"I'll take one, but I'll pay, thanks."

"Let her treat you." Lissa grinned at him, reaching back into the fridge for some full-cream milk. "Makes her feel loved and wanted. 'Pig swill', though, Trev? That's a bit harsh."

Trev snorted. "Old Jim never learned how to make a decent cup of coffee, and nor has his missus. Doesn't want to."

"Old dogs and new tricks," Lissa said. She nodded at Georgie. "Meet my brother's girlfriend, Georgie."

Georgie grinned at him, liking him immediately. "Hi, Trev."

"G'day." The lines around his hazel eyes deepened as he smiled and shook her hand heartily. "In Yamba for a holiday?"

"For about three weeks," Georgie said. "Maybe even longer. We're flexible. And from what we've seen so far, we may never want to leave."

"Yeah, Yamba has that effect on people."

"Trev's a carpenter," Lissa told Georgie. "Helped us with some of the work when we first moved in."

"Bit of a Jack of All Trades, you might say," Trev said. His attention was caught by movement outside the door, and he snorted. "Watch out, Lissa. Your favorite customer is here."

Behind the coffee machine, Lissa looked to see who

was coming and muttered something unintelligible. She handed Trev his coffee and a cupcake, and the two of them exchanged a glance as he handed over a ten-dollar bill.

Lissa waved away payment in disgust. "Don't be silly, Trev. You've helped us out a dozen times."

"Yeah, and you've lost money while you've been closed, haven't you? Take it." Ignoring Lissa's protests, Trev stuffed the money in the tips jar and departed, holding the door open for a stout woman in a floral shirt and wide three-quarter length pants, clutching a bulging brown leather handbag. "G'day there, Irene. How's life treating you?"

"Oh, you know, could be better." She didn't look at him as she barged past, and Trev barely moved his coffee out of the way in time. He widened his eyes at Lissa, mouthed *"Good luck,"* and went on his way.

*Irene*, Georgie thought. Had Lissa mentioned Irene?

"Well, so you're open again." Irene dumped her handbag on a table and moved up to the display cabinet, studying the offerings. "Janet is meeting me here for coffee. To show there are no hard feelings." She sent Lissa a challenging look. "But you know, cockroaches… nasty things. Better to tackle the problem head-on. Can't do that with the cafe open, can you?"

Lissa moved up to stand in front of her on the other side of the counter. "So we should be grateful to you. Is that what you're saying?"

Viv flew out of the kitchen with a determined smile. "Irene! Nice to see you back. Let us treat you to one of Lissa's new banana rum cupcakes. You'll love them." When Irene's gaze moved from Lissa's grim face to the pretty cupcakes, Viv sent Lissa a look heavy with meaning and put a finger to her lips. "Your usual latte? Or are you waiting until Janet gets here?"

"She'll be here any minute; I saw her up the street, outside the bakery. What are the other ones?"

"Apple strudel," Viv said. "Why don't you try one of each and share? If you like them, tell your friends. A new flavor."

"Well, I might just do that." With a narrow-eyed glance at Lissa, Irene took a seat, ignoring Georgie at the next table, and pointed at the door, where a short woman with frizzy curls was coming in. "Here's Janet now."

Leaving them to it, Georgie got up and followed Viv back into the kitchen.

"So," she said. "I'm guessing that Irene is the one who reported you?"

Viv nodded. "Cockroach lady. If Lissa loses her temper with her, she'll go and badmouth us to everyone in the town. We can't afford that. Keep an eye on them, will you?"

"Sure."

Georgie returned to the restaurant. First Amber, then Irene.

It looked like Yamba wasn't going to be quite as peaceful as it had first appeared.

# 5

# Old Jim

MAUREEN BEGGS MOVED a cloth absent-mindedly around the counter, wiping down an already-clean surface, while she watched what was going on across the road. She had to lean forward a little to see properly because *Coffee, Cakes, and Crêpes* wasn't directly opposite, but she had a good enough view.

"I'm sure that's the girls' brother, the one who's just been out setting up tables," she said, loud enough for Jim to hear back in the kitchen. "And that must be his girlfriend, helping out. American, so I hear."

"I'm surprised they reopened," came her husband's voice, heavy with disgust. "What does it take to make people realize they're not wanted?"

Maureen heard a cupboard door slam and the clash of metal pans. She gave an inward sigh. Truth be told, she'd be supremely content if Jim decided to retire and stop obsessing about the opposition across the road. She was tired of waiting tables, tired of cooking fish and chips, tired of getting up every morning to come down and open the cafe.

Not Jim. He'd had this place so long that he wouldn't know what to do with himself if he had to hang around the house.

There were no customers yet, so she kept a running commentary, more for her entertainment than Jim's. "Irene just went in, and Janet's coming down the street. Can you believe it? After Irene went and reported them for cockroaches, she's got the hide to turn up as though nothing had happened."

Jim came out of the kitchen and stood beside her, his hands on his hips. "I'd just as soon the old bag was over there, not here. She's a pain in the rear end."

"A week ago, you were singing her praises," Maureen reminded him. "Said she'd done the right thing by putting in a complaint."

"Yeah, well, if you don't keep your place clean, you've only got yourself to blame."

"I can't help feeling a bit sorry for them. They've had a bad run, what with the power outage and that broken pipe around Christmas." Maureen watched while the girls' brother finished setting up and went inside, then stole a look at Jim, standing there with his eyes narrowed.

She had been annoyed with him for phoning Stan Lambert with a complaint about the extra tables the girls had set up for the crowd last November, but Jim had a bee in his bonnet about people eating out on the footpath. He'd flatly refused to put any seating outside their cafe, even when customers had asked him, and watching customers flocking to *Coffee, Cakes, and Crêpes*, spilling all over the pavement on Melbourne Cup day, had been the last straw.

He was becoming crankier every day, she thought with an inward sigh.

She'd married Jim Beggs for better or for worse, but lately, there'd been way too much of the 'worse'. Still, he *had* agreed to keep sending money to support her sickly mother for the last eighteen months, even though he complained about every dollar he paid out. She knew perfectly well that was only because he had an eye on an inheritance, even though her mother's little 2-bedroom apartment in Maclean wouldn't sell for much.

Her share of the money was due to clear probate any day now, and she still hadn't dared break the news to Jim that her mother had left it to her with the proviso that Jim didn't see a penny of it.

He would be furious, but what did it matter? No matter whose money it was, it would help to ease their retirement in *some* way.

Secretly, she hoped that the cafe across the road would stay open. If their business declined enough, she might—just might—be able to persuade him to retire.

*And pigs might fly.*

"Well," she said, "I'd better have another go at making those fancy coffees that they all want these days." Maureen turned and cast a jaundiced eye at the second-hand coffee machine that she had finally persuaded Jim to buy. Even after taking a couple of sneaky barista classes over at the girls' cafe on a Sunday afternoon when Jim was at golf hadn't helped. She just couldn't get the hang of steaming the milk. "Stretching" the milk, young Lissa had called it. All Maureen could manage was something that looked like soap bubbles.

Her words reminded Jim of money he'd spent on something he didn't want in the first place. He frowned at the machine and shook his head. "I told you not to buy it. Why you'd take the advice of some uppity young girl with dyed hair and tattoos, I'll never know. All a lot of nonsense if you ask me. Nothing wrong with the percolator."

"It's what the customers want," Maureen said defensively. "I'll get the hang of it."

Maureen went to the machine and opened up the instruction book beside it again. It would be kind of nice to have people coming in and saying her coffee was as good as Lissa's.

But for that to happen, she probably needed to go to more classes, and if Jim found out, he'd have a fit.

*Don't close*, she found herself thinking, glancing across at the girls' cafe again. *Stay open and put us out of business.*

With a quick guilty glance at Jim's back, while he was busy crumbing a fish fillet at the kitchen counter, she got to work figuring out what she was doing wrong with the milk.

It seemed that half the locals in Yamba found an excuse to drop by the cafe and try Lissa's new cupcake recipes —and to discuss the cafe closure. Most of them seemed supportive, at least on the surface. A good many were curious, asking not-so-subtle questions. There was a good sprinkling of tourists, too: most of them older people staying in the caravan parks.

Georgie stayed and helped out until after the lunchtime rush, finding that she easily dropped back into the rhythm of waiting tables, her part-time job during her years at college back in the States.

"Thanks," Lissa said when the three of them finally had the chance to sit down over coffee. "I didn't mean for you to come to Yamba so we could put you to work. But we appreciate it."

"I enjoyed it," Georgie said honestly. "But that's because I don't have to do it all the time. Different for you two."

"I thought if one more person asked me if we were going to stay open, I was going to throw something," confessed Lissa. "But I was conscious of Viv frowning at me from the kitchen. And as for *Irene…*" She made strangling motions with her hands.

"Throttling Irene Wilson isn't going to help," Viv pointed out. "Or insulting her."

"Maybe not, but it would make me *feel* better." Lissa sat back in her chair and rolled her shoulders. "At least the cupcakes were a success. You'll be baking again tonight. But don't worry, I'll help."

Viv sat back in her chair and looked at Georgie. "I don't suppose…." She hesitated, thinking through what she wanted to say.

"Sure, I'll help too," Georgie jumped in. "Can't say I ever tried baking cupcakes before, but I can follow orders."

"No, no. Not the cupcakes; I can bake those in my sleep. What I was going to say is—well, working here this morning, watching everyone coming in and out of the cafe, I don't suppose you've got any insights?" Viv opened her hands out. "Like, you didn't look at anyone coming in and think: *That's him! That's the bad guy!*"

Georgie and Lissa both had to laugh at her expression.

"I'd love to be able to say yes," Georgie said. "But —" She shrugged. "Not a thing. Sorry."

Lissa leaned forward. "What about if you used your crystal ball? Do you think you might see anything then?"

"I did take a quick peek," Georgie admitted, "When we got back to our caravan the first night we were here after you told us about all your problems."

"And?" Lissa asked, and both sisters looked at her curiously.

"Nothing helpful. A lot of what's happened to you could happen to anybody—but not *all* of it. That's the feeling you've got, and that's the feeling I have as well."

Lissa looked down at her plate, now empty but for a few crumbs of one of the slices from the bakery. She said nothing but nodded, looking a little discouraged.

Viv put her elbow on the table and leaned one cheek on her fist. "What about now? Now that you met some of the locals? And what if we were there while you did a reading? Would that make a difference?"

"It probably would," Georgie said. "It sure can't hurt to try."

"Tonight?" Lissa asked hopefully.

"Tonight would be great," Georgie said. "If you're going to be busy making cupcakes, I'll bring the crystal ball over, and we can do a reading while you're waiting for them to bake."

"Done. After that, we can relax and have a drink to celebrate our grand reopening," Viv said. "I'll pick up some wine."

"We'll come early and bring food," Georgie said. "Everyone like Thai?"

Everyone nodded, so with that settled, Georgie left them to their afternoon trade and headed off.

It was time to see what Scott had been up to while she'd been helping out at the cafe. He had planned to contact his brother Bluey to see what information he could ferret out about Stan Lambert and Amber Kaye. Georgie was curious to see if their friendly family hacker had found anything.

Walking down the street back to the caravan park, she felt surprisingly cheerful.

*The thrill of the chase.* It was on again… finding out why things were going wrong and who was behind it. When she and a few friends back in the States had formed their 'Crystal Ball Investigation Team' it had been more of a joke than anything else until they started solving cases.

Now, half a world away, she had a new team. The thought of her rag-tag group of "investigators" brought a smile to her face. Georgie the eighth-generation gypsy and her crystal ball, Scott, his brother Bluey-the-Hacker, and his mother Louise, who did horoscopes for a living and read cards on the side.

Not exactly a group that a proper investigation team would take seriously, but they did okay for amateurs.

Not for the first time, she wondered what life might have been like if she'd decided to be a *real* detective.

$$\frac{6}{}$$

## Kayaks and Crystal Balls

WHEN GEORGIE GOT BACK to their campsite, she found Scott with his head halfway inside a yellow kayak while he reached forward to adjust something out of sight. A short distance away, she could see an identical kayak in blue.

She put her hands on her hips. "So this is what you get up to when I turn my back for half a day?"

He sat up and grinned at her. "Just in time. Come and sit in this while I finish adjusting the pedals." He stood up and wiped his hands on his shorts. "I took a guess at it, but I think this should be about right for you."

"We're going kayaking?" Georgie kicked off her sandals and stepped inside the kayak, wriggling into position on the seat. "This could end badly. I'm not exactly experienced."

"You managed okay with the canoes back in the States, and these are more streamlined. Easier to control. Here, lean forward."

Georgie wriggled forward, and Scott tightened the

straps on the backrest to bring it forward a little. "Okay. Sit back. How does that feel?"

"Good. Comfortable." Georgie peered down into the kayak and put her feet on the pedals, bunching her skirt up around her knees. "Does this look right?"

"You should be sitting with your knees slightly bent. That way, you can brace against the sides of the kayak if you need to." Scott stood back with his hands on his hips and assessed her position. "That doesn't look too bad. Want to get changed? Go out and give them a try?"

Georgie laughed. "Something tells me that I'm going to be in for a ducking." She tilted her head back and looked up at the perfect blue sky. "Great day for it, though."

"You can learn in shallow water, figure out the basics here…you'll pick it up more as we travel."

Georgie looked at him. "As we travel? They're *ours?* I thought you must have hired them."

"Yep." Scott extended a hand to haul her up out of the kayak. "This is your Yamba present." He nodded at the LandCruiser, which now sported new roof racks with kayak cradles. "Had those installed this morning. I'll show you how to load the kayaks and tie them down later. For now, we'll just go and paddle around down there." He waved at the quiet waters of the river, visible from their site.

"What fun!" This was just what Georgie needed after being on her feet most of the day in the cafe; sunshine and fresh air.

Time enough to worry about sabotage and nasty people tonight, after she'd had time to clear her head.

That night, satisfyingly full of Thai food and with the heavenly scent of cupcakes cooling on the kitchen counter, they all settled down with a glass of wine around the dining table, with the crystal ball in the center.

"I can't believe I'm going to see you in action at last." Lissa leaned forward, with her elbows on the table and her fingers linked around the stem of her wine glass. "I mean, we're all used to watching Mum read the cards, and Scott too, once he got into it—but a crystal ball? That's different."

They were sitting in the flickering light of three fat candles resting on the nearby window sill. The only light Georgie had left on was over the kitchen cooktop, so the dining table was bathed in a soft radiance.

Viv studied the crystal ball with her head on one side, her blue-grey eyes serious. "I feel kind of nervous. How crazy is that?"

"A lot of people do if they've never had a reading before." Georgie grinned at her. "Don't worry; you're amongst friends here. Some of the people that I've done readings for had something to hide, and that can make things awkward."

Lissa stood up and faked consternation. "And you think I *don't*? My parents would be in an early grave if they had any idea of some of the things I did overseas. I'm outta here."

Laughing, Scott pulled her back down again. "Don't worry; we're not going to rat on you."

Lissa made a face. "I don't even want my *brother* knowing what I got up to."

"I don't think there's too much to worry about," Georgie assured her, amused. "As long as you're not on the run for some terrible crime. Anyway, it's not like I'm going to see your whole life laid out in front of me, like reading a book."

"Quite the opposite, sometimes," Scott put in. "It's like *'Who, me, psychic? You must be thinking someone else.'*"

"And that could well be the case tonight." Georgie drew the crystal ball closer. "I guess the question is whether all this is just your everyday series of disasters… or is someone gunning for you?"

"I have a feeling it'll be a mix of both," Scott said. "Which will probably make it harder to work out who's behind it."

Georgie glanced from Lissa, with her whiskey-colored eyes like Scott's, to Viv, who looked more like her mother. *Please let me find something to help them,* she said silently. For a brief moment, she thought of Rosa, her great-grandmother, and wondered if she could sense what was happening, all those miles away. Georgie often thought that Rosa had left a lot of herself in the crystal ball.

It would be nice to think that she was sitting in her little sunroom at Elkhart, looking out at the snow and thinking of Georgie, reaching out across the ocean.

It was entirely possible. Rosa and Scott's mother regularly talked on the phone.

Georgie smoothed her palm across the surface of the crystal ball. "I don't want to dictate what you should do, or think, or say," she told them. "You probably have questions in your mind related to all of this. It might be as simple as 'who did it?' or it might be 'is so-and-so involved?'"

"Like Stan Lambert," said Lissa. "Or Amber."

"Anyone. You'll probably find different ideas or questions floating into your mind while we sit here."

"It sounds a bit like meditation," Lissa said. "Are we allowed to talk while this is happening? Or should we just wait and see what you have to tell us?"

"Let's just play it by ear," Georgie suggested. "You might or might not see anything in the crystal ball, by the way. Everyone is different."

She was conscious of their eyes flicking from the crystal ball to her face, and then she shut them all out, because the crystal surface was starting to grow warm under her fingers.

*Good,* she thought, with a tiny flicker of relief. When she felt that temperature change, there was usually something coming through.

Would it be images? Words? Feelings? She never knew.

She waited, and this time, she saw first the familiar mist forming in the crystal ball and then some dark shapes.

Lots of small, scuttling dark shapes. She frowned and stared. Were they...*cockroaches?*

They were.

Georgie looked up with a wry grin and found Lissa leaning forward, staring intently, her mouth dropping open. She waited until the other girl's head jerked up, and she met Georgie's eyes. "Am I seeing what I think I'm seeing?"

"Cockroaches?"

"Jeez," Lissa said. "As though it's not enough to have to cope with the little buggers at work, now they're invading your crystal ball."

"Well, not literally, thank goodness."

Viv looked frustrated. "I can't see anything. Why can't I see them?"

"Close your eyes," Georgie suggested, still staring at the moving shapes. "You might be someone who senses things rather than sees them. Be open for feelings, maybe words coming into your mind." She held up a hand. "Wait, is that…?" She looked closer and then back up at Lissa. "What do you see?"

Lissa frowned. "A hand?"

A hand, Georgie thought, with cockroaches trickling in a short stream from the hand to the floor. She looked at Scott. "Scott…?"

Scott met her eyes and nodded. He had interpreted what he saw exactly as she had. "Yes. A hand."

Lissa looked at them both and made the connection. "A *hand*. Someone *did* bring them in, didn't they? *Crap.*" Fury sparked in her eyes. "That rotting piece of fish, I was certain that someone must have planted that, unless a darned cat or something brought it in, but how would a cat get in? But the cockroaches…I know what I said to the landlord about them, but that was because I was so mad at him. I really thought we were just unlucky, that there was a plague of them or something. Indestructible, nuclear-explosion-proof roaches. But this—!" She ran out of words, her eyes moving from Scott to Georgie to her sister. "Who would do that? *Who?*"

Viv had opened her eyes again, frowning at not being able to see what they could, but not doubting it for a moment. "You saw that for sure? Someone brought in cockroaches?"

"That's the interpretation I'm putting on this,"

Georgie said slowly. "It feels right." She nodded at Viv. "What do you feel?"

"What Lissa said. We've been paranoid with pest control. But with cockroaches, you're never on top. That's why it didn't occur to us that it could be…" she looked at her sister. "Not Irene. She's a cow, but she wouldn't deliberately seed the place with cockroaches and then report them, would she?"

"I doubt it. What would she have to gain?"

"It depends," Scott said, "whether she's friends with someone else who wants you out. Would she do that for anybody else?"

For a moment, Lissa and Viv were silent, but they shook their heads almost at the same time.

"Don't think so," said Viv. Then her eyes grew speculative. "But…what about Amber?"

"Huh." Lissa sat up. "She hates you, and if you want my opinion, she's still concerned that Shane might decide that he's made a huge mistake and wants you back. Yes, I could imagine *her* doing it."

"Even if he did decide he'd made a mistake," Viv said shortly, "It's too late. That's done and dusted." She sat, thinking. "Amber… hmmm. Maybe. Maybe."

Scott tapped his fingers on the table. "Today, Amber came by just before Irene Wilson arrived." His eyes went to Viv. "For it to work, Amber would have to time it right. Cockroaches are like lightning. They scuttle away, hide. She'd almost have to be there at the same time as Irene. Would that have been likely?"

"Irene does tend to come early when we open. Then she and Janet go on to a craft morning or a council meeting or any of six other pies she has a finger in."

"Okay, then." Scott raised his eyebrows. "Looks like

we have suspect number one, then. Amber. What about Stan Lambert?"

"He seems keen for us to go to this other complex," Lissa pointed out. "But he never comes into the cafe, so he couldn't have introduced the cockroaches."

"But he does have a key," Viv said.

"In that case, let's add him to the shortlist. Two suspects, Stan Lambert and Amber whatever her name is."

"Amber Kaye," Viv said.

"Amber Kaye. Anyone else? Who else comes in early?"

"Lots of people pick up an early morning cup of coffee on their way somewhere," Lissa admitted. "They're in and out."

"Okay," he said. "Georgie, are you picking up anything else?"

"Yes," Georgie said reluctantly. "I'm not *seeing* anything else, but I am getting a feeling about things—a fairly *definite* feeling. Sorry, guys. But I don't think you're looking for one person. I think there are several people behind all this."

---

7

# Shadows in the Night

---

THE MOWBRAY SISTERS' No. 1 Enemy (as he liked to think of himself) allowed them a few nights to grow complacent before he made his next move. Months before, he'd searched online for 'ways to sabotage a café', and now it was time for the next item on his list. It blew his brain what inventive ideas discontented workers could come up with.

At three or four in the morning, most of the world was asleep. He slipped past the bakery, where a crack of light showed under the blinds on a back window. Shane Carter's white van was parked out front, with Amber Kaye's little silver hatchback next to it.

He'd heard the stories about Shane and Amber. That little bit of gossip had been an unexpected bonus, an extra incentive for the older Mowbray sister to want to sell up and get out of town.

When you thought about it, who could blame Shane? A stacked blonde firecracker like Amber versus that skinny older sister with her serious face? No contest.

He moved quietly down the street and went around the back of *Coffee, Cakes & Crepes*. After a quick look around to check that he wasn't being observed, he let himself in.

This must be getting on for half a dozen visits over the past four months, and they were still rabbiting on to customers about a run of bad luck. It couldn't go on for much longer; he understood that. Either they'd wise up, or they'd close.

But for now, he was still AOK. So, time to execute tonight's plan.

He'd contemplated engineering another health scare, but it was a bit too close to the cockroach incident. It was only a few days since they'd reopened, and they'd be paranoid, checking every corner of the place each day. That could wait a week or two.

He couldn't stop a smile at the thought of the cockroaches. That had worked perfectly: Irene had talked about her experience long and loud to anyone who'd listen—the butcher, the gift shop, the Post Office staff, Maureen, and finally the council.

So, no pests tonight.

No broken pipes.

No monkeying about with the wiring.

Tonight was simple, but it would give them a few more headaches.

One thing after another, like a drip on a stone.

Drip, drip, drip.

He got to work, and within ten minutes, was letting himself out again with the things he'd purloined, slipping away through the silent streets.

$$\overline{\hspace{6cm}}$$

8

## Losing It

$$\overline{\hspace{6cm}}$$

GEORGIE DECIDED to spend a few hours in the cafe each morning for the three weeks they were visiting. For one thing, Viv and Lissa could do with the help. Money was tight, and they hadn't yet employed another backpacker to take Lissa's place when she was running weekly barista classes in Maclean and Grafton.

Secondly, she wanted to get a sense of who came into the cafe, both locals and visitors. Maybe the saboteur would be among them, and if he or she did, she *might* pick up something.

On the third day after the cafe had reopened, after a few hours' intensive training from the Coffee Whisperer, aka Lissa, she tied on an apron and took her place behind the coffee machine.

"You're this morning's guinea pig," she told Scott when he came in from setting up the tables outside. "Long black? Flat white? Cappuccino? Latte? Name your poison."

"Long black's no challenge," came Viv's voice from the kitchen. "You need practice in stretching the milk."

"No worries," Scott said, lounging back comfortably in a corner booth. "I've already decided. I'll have a caramel macchiato, thanks. Large."

Georgie put her hands on her hips. "You will not. You hate sweet coffee."

"Yeah, but I need to challenge you. This barista business isn't for the faint-hearted, you know." He smiled at her lazily.

"Give him a large cappuccino," Viv said. "And I'll have a latte."

"Right. Here we go." Georgie looked for the handle with the metal cup, but it wasn't there.

It wasn't in the cupboards, either. Or anywhere on the workspace.

She went to the kitchen, where Viv was unpacking today's cupcakes. "Viv? I can't find the thing you put the coffee grounds into. Is it out here?"

"What thing?" Viv looked up in puzzlement. "A container?"

"No, the handle thing that locks into the machine."

"Oh, the portafilter. It's in the cupboard."

Georgie shook her head. "No, it isn't. Did Lissa wash it up last night? When she was getting stuff ready for her class today?"

"She always puts it back." Viv went back into the shop with her, but within minutes they were looking at each other in a panic. "You're right. It's not there."

Scott stood up. "What's missing?"

"Only the most essential part of the machine." Viv was already tapping the fast-dial button to Lissa on her phone. "She probably won't answer; she doesn't while she's driving."

"She needs Bluetooth."

"I know, it's one of those things we keep meaning to do…no, she's not answering. I'll send a text."

There was a light rap of knuckles at the door, and Trev came in, ignoring the 'closed' sign as usual. "G'day all. How're things?" He beamed at Georgie, already aware that she was the barista-in-training. "OK, Georgie, do your thing. I'll give you a score out of ten like Lissa, only I'll be more generous."

"You'd be generous all right," Georgie said, her heart rate accelerating. Scott's sisters *so* didn't need this, on top of everything else. "There's a bit missing on the machine, and we can't contact Lissa."

"What kind of bit?" Always ready to offer mechanical expertise, Trev moved to the back of the machine. "Something broken?"

"No, it's a proper part of it. The bit you put the coffee in. The handle thing."

"Ah, I know." Trev nodded. "Can't help you there. It'll turn up. I'll just take a carton of chocolate milk, then. I'm not desperate enough to go over and get Maureen's coffee."

"OK." Georgie shot a glance at the clock on the wall. "Irene and Janet will be here in about fifteen minutes. We *can't* not be operating."

"That's for sure." Viv turned to Scott. "Scotty, back at our place, there's our good machine on the kitchen counter, and two others in the laundry, on the shelf. Can you hot-foot it over there and pick them up?"

"I'm gone." As good as his word, Scott flew out of the door.

Trev scanned the faces in front of him as Georgie handed him his carton of flavored milk. "You going to be all right?"

"Sure," Viv said, her voice lacking conviction. "We'll get through. Here, take a muffin with you."

"I'll get fat," he protested, but took one anyway, his hazel eyes smiling at her. When she couldn't muster up a smile in return, he squeezed her shoulder comfortingly. "You girls can't take a trick, can you? Hang in there, Vivi. Lissa's probably got the missing bit with her; she'll phone up full of apologies."

"Thanks Trev." She gave him a grateful smile, watching him go, and said to Georgie, "Salt of the earth. I wish there were more like him."

Two minutes later, right on schedule, Amber breezed in, juggling a tray. "Hello, hello! A dozen vanilla slices, Shane's special fruit loaf, some carrot cake and a torte, as ordered." She flashed her wide fake smile and sashayed past them, straight to the kitchen.

Georgie and Viv exchanged a look and followed her. Until she could be ruled out, they had decided to watch every move Amber made. So far, there had been no sign of a further sneaky deposit of cockroaches, but who knew what else she might have in mind?

Amber stood and watched while Viv stacked the bakery items on separate smaller trays, her eyes moving inquisitively around the kitchen. "All back on track now? No sign of creepy crawlies?"

*Not other than you,* Georgie felt like saying, but seeing Viv's teeth clench, she stepped in. "Clean as a whistle. Just as it always is."

Amber's eyes fixed on hers, and this time there was a hint of spite in her gaze. "Well, not *quite* always. But I have to give it to you, you could eat off the floor in here this morning."

"You could," Viv agreed. "And I must say, in all fairness, I've seen the bakery when it's less than pristine, Amber."

"Not since I arrived," Amber said. "But you haven't been there for a while, so you wouldn't know." She leaned back and rested her elbows on the preparation area behind her, a move which displayed her generous cleavage to advantage in her low-cut t-shirt. The white cotton was thin enough to show a hint of lace underneath.

Amber saw Viv notice, and gave a little cat-like smile.

"That's true," Viv said evenly. "I haven't been to the bakery because I've been flat out running a business. And since I like to keep things hygienic, would you mind taking your elbows off my food prep area?"

Amber's smile disappeared. She stepped away from the counter, watching Viv swab the counter with alcohol wipes. "Now you're being petty."

"Now I'm being *careful*," Viv said, stripping off her thin plastic gloves and replacing them with a fresh set from the box on the counter. She dropped the used gloves in a pedal bin and met Amber's gaze challengingly as she handed her the empty tray. "Here. Thanks."

Amber took the tray, but didn't move. "Where's Lissa today?"

"Running a class in Grafton."

"Have you hired another backpacker?"

"She doesn't need to," Georgie said. "She has family here."

Amber nodded, looking her up and down. "You've had experience in this sort of thing?"

"I've been trained by the best," Georgie said. "Worked all over the States." All of which was true, even though none of her work in the States had been as a barista. "And now I'd better get to work."

Amber followed her out of the door. "That sounds impressive. Tell you what, I'll take two coffees to go. I'll have a latte. Shane has—"

"Sorry," Georgie said before Viv had a chance to respond. "We're not actually open yet. You could come back later, or I'll bring it to you. As a special favor, seeing we're all supporting local businesses."

Amber frowned. "I see Trev come in here every morning before you're open and walk out with a coffee."

"Trev's a friend," Viv said coolly. "We'll bring them down within half an hour, Amber. If you still want them?"

Looking annoyed, Amber hesitated, but then nodded. "Sure. I want to see what kind of a job your newest staff member does. If her coffee is as good as she says, I'll make sure word gets around."

"I didn't say it was good," Georgie pointed out. "Just that I'd been trained by the best. But I have confidence."

"Fine." Amber turned and walked out, a hint of petulance in her stride. "Later, then."

They watched her go, and Georgie saw Viv's hands clench into fists. "She makes me *homicidal.*"

"Be grateful for small mercies," Georgie said, seeing Scott pull into a space outside. "She just missed seeing Scott bring in the replacement machines. *That* would have been gossip fodder. Now I've got to make two of the best cups of coffee I've ever made. On *domestic* machines."

Viv let out a strangled laugh. "You can do it. You weren't lying. You really have been trained by the best."

"True," Georgie said, opening the door for Scott. "I

just wish it had been for more than a couple of hours. But at least Amber didn't drop a colony of cockroaches onto the floor. We've got to be in front."

No cockroaches, she thought. But an essential part of the coffee machine missing?

Bad. Very bad.

9

## Talk of the Town

Fifteen minutes later, for better or worse, Georgie had made one cappuccino and one latte for the Bakery Apprentice from Hell. Well, actually, she'd made two of each: Lissa and Scott had acted as guinea pigs with the first lot.

"The coffee is fine," Viv pronounced. "Honestly, even Lissa would rate it an eight, and that's high praise. Especially made with a machine snatched from our kitchen at home. Go, take it to her while it's hot. I'll hold the fort."

Georgie loaded the cardboard cups into a takeout tray, along with two of Viv's raspberry and cream muffins, and held up crossed fingers. "Wish me luck."

"Lighten up. You're not going to war," Scott said.

"Taking home-cooked muffins to the town bakery? Gotta run a close second." Georgie pushed her way out of the door, glanced up and down the street, and said over her shoulder, "Can't see Irene and Janet yet. I'll be back ASAP."

She hurried down the road, took a deep breath, and walked into the bakery.

Immediately, she gave a silent groan.

*That* was why Irene and Janet hadn't shown up yet. They were down here, making mischief and spreading gossip, led by Amber. The three of them were in a huddle at the end of the counter, along with two other women, and Georgie caught "…tried to tell me that the *bakery* was less than pristine! I mean, look at it! Can you—" At that point, Amber looked up to see who was coming in and stopped speaking.

"Georgie!" she said brightly. "I thought you said half an hour."

"*Within* half an hour, I think Viv said." Georgie plastered on a confident smile and walked over to them all. "Hi Irene, Janet," she said. "Buying up some of Shane's award-winning slices?" She put the takeout tray on the counter. "I brought a couple of Viv's cupcakes for you to try, Amber. Incredibly delicious! Raspberry and cream. She's added a secret ingredient." Georgie mimicked zipping her lips. "Can't tell you what it is, or she'll kill me." Turning to the two women she hadn't met, she grinned. "Hi, I'm Georgie. I have to say; I love your town. The people are so friendly."

"Hello," said a tall, thin woman with a curly mop of salt-and-pepper hair and twinkling eyes. "I'm Adele. And I'll have one of Viv's cupcakes any time." She indicated the woman with her, a shorter and rounder version of herself with a similarly friendly face. "My sister, Chris."

"Hi." Chris moved closer to peer at the cupcakes. "They look too good to eat."

"Exactly what I tell Viv every time she turns out a

new batch. The woman's obsessed. I think she's deter-mined to set the record for the widest variety of cupcakes available in a country cafe." Georgie cast a laughing glance at Amber. "Note I said *cafe*, Amber, not *bakery*."

Amber looked put out, which had not gone unno-ticed by Irene and Janet. Out of the corner of her eye, Georgie caught them exchanging a smirk.

Continuing the momentum, she pointed to the card-board cups. "I hope you enjoy the coffee, Amber. Want to taste it now? Give me your verdict?" She put a dramatic hand to her forehead. "I promise not to cry if you say you hate it."

Amber compressed her lips and snatched one of the cups.

"Oh, that's Shane's," Georgie said. "Viv told me just how he likes his cappuccino. You wanted a latte, right? You don't take sweetener, according to Viv."

"That's right." Amber put the first cup down on the counter a little too forcefully, so that some cream oozed out of the spout, and took the other one. With them all watching, she had no choice but to sample it.

Georgie almost laughed, watching the expression on her face as she weighed up what to say. Amber was canny enough to know that she might lose ground if she was rude.

"Not as good as Lissa's, I know," Georgie said modestly. "There's a reason she's so much in demand. But—well, I used to have my share of devoted customers."

That wasn't *exactly* a lie, except her devoted customers were all buyers of vintage RVs.

Amber made a decision and put a game face on

things. "Georgie, it's excellent! Well *done!*" She put up a hand for a high-five and drank some more. "It's a pity you're not staying in Yamba. With the cafe in so much trouble, they could do with you there to help out."

*Oooh. The sucker punch.*

"Thanks," Georgie said. "I'd better be getting back. I don't want to leave Viv short-handed. I hope Shane enjoys his, too."

"Hope Shane enjoys his what?" A tall male emerged from a room at the back, nodding at the group. "Ladies. How are we all this morning?" His eyes found Georgie, the stranger in the group, and then his gaze moved to the cupcakes and coffee.

Well, thought Georgie. No wonder Amber had been tempted to get her hooks into him. Shane was tall and well-built with blonde good looks and an open, friendly face. His apron was dusted with flour or maybe icing sugar.

"Your coffee," Georgie said in answer to his question. "Lissa's in Grafton today, so I'm your friendly barista."

Amber handed him the cappuccino, maintaining the lighthearted facade. "Yours."

"Thanks." His eyes met Georgie's briefly before he looked away, a hint of embarrassment in his eyes now he knew who she was.

Georgie could read him as clearly as if his personality had been analyzed by a bunch of psychologists and a dozen card-readers and fortune-tellers all working together and comparing notes.

A harmless, good-natured, good-looking guy who would always take the easy road. Weak, she thought. He would end up hurting people just because he couldn't say no, in the same way he'd hurt Viv rather than reject Amber.

He was no loss to Viv, and one day when she'd stopped smarting over it all, Georgie would tell her that.

Or maybe she wouldn't have to. Viv was smart enough to work it out for herself.

There was one thing she knew immediately: Shane Carter was not behind what was happening to *Coffee, Cakes & Crepes.* Amber…maybe. She was mean enough. Whether she was clever enough to engineer everything that had happened to Lissa and Viv, Georgie wasn't sure.

Hmm. She was certain that more than one person was involved. Amber could easily be working with someone else.

Anyway. They could cross *one* off the list. Not Shane. She was glad about that, for Viv's sake.

"Hey, this is good." Shane nodded and tipped the coffee cup toward her in acknowledgment. "I might come up for another at lunchtime."

Georgie arched her eyebrows. "Plus one of the town's best cupcakes?"

"Have to test them first." Falling easily into flirt mode, Shane winked at her.

"We might see you later, then." Georgie nodded at everyone. "I have to run."

"Wait," Irene said. "We'll walk back with you."

"Us, too," said Adele. "We'll have to go snag some of those cupcakes before they're all gone." She picked up her shopping bag. "See you, Amber. Shane."

Oh great, Georgie thought. Four people for coffee, and one machine out of action.

Help.

# 10

# Maureen Asks for Help

THAT AFTERNOON, just as the four of them sat down to have a council of war after *Coffee, Cakes & Crepes* had closed for the day, there was a tap on the door.

Looking up to yell out, "We're closed!" Lissa saw that it was Maureen Beggs from across the road.

She sighed. "What now? If Jim Beggs has another gripe, I swear I'll go over there and choke him."

"He won't be there," Viv said, slumped in a chair, looking frazzled after the frantic day coping with customers without a commercial coffee machine. "It's his golf afternoon."

"He always gets Maureen to do his dirty work anyway." Lissa got up and went over to the door. When she saw Maureen's nervous expression, she forced a smile to her face. There was no need to make her life any harder than it was.

"Hi, Maureen. What can I do for you?"

Maureen cast a look over her shoulder as though fearful that Jim could somehow see her even from the golf club. "I was just wondering…you know I did that coffee course with you?"

Lissa did indeed know. Maureen had been one of the most clueless people she'd ever tried to train. Her coffee was legendary for all the wrong reasons.

"Yes?" Lissa smiled encouragingly.

"I don't think I've quite got the hang of it yet. I was hoping—are you still doing that Sunday afternoon class?"

"I sure am."

Maureen's voice dropped to almost a whisper, looking past Lissa to where the other three sat waiting for her. "Is there room for me? This Sunday, while Jim's playing golf?"

"Of course," Lissa said. "Three o'clock. I'd love to have you."

Maureen went to open her handbag. "I can pay you now."

"No, no." Lissa waved it away. "Sunday's fine."

"Thank you." Maureen looked relieved. "I just know I can learn if I practice enough. And today, everyone was saying how your American visitor is another expert, and her coffee's really good. Is she going to be there?"

Lissa choked back a laugh. "I'll ask her." She turned and could tell by the carefully blank expressions on the others' faces that they'd heard. "Georgie, as our American expert, are you going to be helping out at the class on Sunday?" She batted her eyelashes. "Maybe even *running* it, if we're lucky?"

"Sure," Georgie said weakly. "Uh, I'll be there."

Maureen gave her a tiny wave, and the nervous smile came back. "I'm not saying anything to Jim. He thinks the old ways are best, and, um…."

"And he's not exactly a fan of ours." Lissa winked and patted Maureen on the arm to take the sting out of her words. "We won't breathe a word, Maureen. But you should know that Irene and Janet have booked in too."

In other words, the biggest gossip in town and her sidekick were going to be right there standing next to her.

Maureen's face fell. "Oh."

"On the other hand," Lissa said, "If you told them you wanted to keep it a *secret* from Jim, I'm sure they would." She laughed. "You know there's nothing they like better than being entrusted with a secret."

A tiny flash of humor entered Maureen's eyes. "You're right about that. Well…see you on Sunday."

Lissa stayed at the door and watched her walk away a few steps and then, on impulse, called her name. "Maureen?"

The other woman turned, her eyes immediately wary again. "Yes?"

"Can I just ask you…oh, heck, I'll just say it. Your Jim. Why's he so set against us?"

Maureen looked painfully embarrassed. "It's not really you. It's anything modern. All these coffees and teas and…and cakes with names like *"friands"*, and—" Her gaze skated over the tattoo on Lissa's bicep and flicked up to her vibrant orange hair. "Anything kind of alternative, I guess."

Lissa saw where she was looking. "And I'm about as alternative as you can get. It's okay, Maureen, I understand." Lissa still leaned on the door and debated about the next question but asked it anyway. "Do you think he'd be happy if we closed down? Shut the shop completely?"

Conflicting expressions fought on Maureen's face. "Jim just wants everything to stay the same as it's been for the last twenty-five years. Him messing around in the kitchen, having a yarn with the men who call in, playing golf two days a week." Her voice suddenly gained strength. "With me cooking fish and chips and serving instant coffee or tea. I *don't* want that. I want to retire, go to craft days like Irene and Janet and Adele." Her voice lowered. "So please don't close down."

"Oh." Lissa blinked.

"He's paranoid about having enough money to support us in our retirement. Silly man, we don't need much." She waved that off. "Meanwhile, can you just teach me how to make coffee the way you do it here? Until I *can* retire." Then, seeing Lissa's expression, Maureen backed away as though she'd said too much. "Sorry. It's just been a long day. Golf days are good because I get a break from Jim, but I get tired on my own."

"I thought Jim was hiring backpackers for a couple of hours a day?"

"Now and then. He has them for a while, and it's all right, and then he goes through a phase of "I'm not having those lazy buggers taking part of the profits," and it's just the two of us again." She took another few steps away. "I've got to lock up, go home and cook something. I'll see you on Sunday."

"I'll look forward to it," Lissa said, feeling sorry for her.

She watched her walk away, clearly tired and unhappy.

As you would be, married to cranky old Jim Beggs.

However, it didn't sound as though they could blame Jim for the plague of cockroaches. He'd never set foot in their place, other than reluctantly showing them through when they were on the hunt for suitable premises when Stan Lambert and his wife were overseas.

"Hey, Liss. You coming?" came Viv's voice from behind her.

Lissa closed the door, locked it, and went back to join the others.

"Right," she said. "The mystery of the missing portafilter. Something's pretty darn fishy."

---

In the early hours of the next morning, the Mowbray Sister's No. 1 Enemy was extra careful about not being seen. He'd paid special attention to what was being said around the town about the goings-on at *Coffee, Cakes & Crepes*, but apparently, they'd made up some cover story about demonstrating how home coffee machines really could produce restaurant-quality coffee, to promote their barista classes.

That just went to show that people would believe anything.

He waited in the shadowy backyard for a long time, watching and waiting, alert for any signs that someone was lying in wait inside the cafe. If they suspected that someone was breaking in, surely someone would be keeping an eye on the place? Like that young bloke Scott. He wanted to make sure he didn't run into *him*.

A dog would have been the best solution, shut in the

backyard, ready to raise the roof if anyone came. If it had been him, *he'd* have thought of a dog.

Finally, he decided that there was nobody inside, and within the space of a few minutes was in and out again, putting back the things he'd removed the night before—but not in the same place: he wanted them scratching their heads, thinking they'd just mislaid them.

Outside, he padded silently away, removing his thin polyethylene gloves and stuffing them back in his pocket.

*That* was done.

Already, he was planning his next move. Mice perhaps?

He'd need an offsider for that.

# 11

# Kayaking Insights

GEORGIE WATCHED Scott closely as he skimmed along the water ten feet ahead of her, dipping his paddle in first one side and then the other.

Effortless, she thought. No splashing; he looked like a well-oiled machine.

How did he do that twist thing with his hands in mid-air when the paddle was moving from one side to the other? It rotated somehow through his palm.

*Her* hand was cramping from gripping the paddle, and she wished she had gloves to stop the rubbing.

No doubt it was all practice, like everything else.

Scott slowed, rested his paddle across the kayak, and turned to wait for her. Georgie narrowly avoided smashing right into him.

"How's it going? Want to pull over to the side for a while, get out and rest on the shore?"

"Okay, yes and yes." She grimaced. "How come this looks so easy when you do it, but it's not?"

"You're doing okay. Just follow me in. Paddle quickly and let the momentum carry it up onto the sand."

He headed straight for the small strip of sand, and the kayak coasted in, scraping on the sand before it stopped. Scott got out, dragged it up further, and then watched while she followed him in, skewing sideways.

"Not bad." He steadied the kayak while she clambered out and then peeled back the rubber hatch to pull out the wet sack with their sandwiches.

Georgie stretched and sat down thankfully. "My legs have cramps. My hands have cramps. My lower *back* has cramps."

"I know you're keen, but two hours was probably too much for your first proper paddle."

"I know, I know, you told me so." Georgie leaned back against a tree trunk where the scrub met the grass.

Scott handed her a sandwich and a bottle of water. "We'll get in a few practice sessions while we're here, so you can start feeling comfortable. Paddle around Crystal Lake and in and out of the canals. It's nice paddling along the Esk River, too."

Georgie nibbled at her sandwich and stared out at the sparkling waters of Yamba Bay. Scott had said it was a good place to start, and it was, she supposed.

Had the canoes back on the West Coast of the States been this much of a challenge?

No, because she'd just messed about in them, in and out in fifteen minutes, and laughing about her lack of expertise with a paddle.

Now she was in something longer and sleeker with a rudder and a life jacket that felt bulky and odd. What had Scott called it? Something about flotation. PFD, that was it. Personal Flotation Device. She tugged it down a little. PSJ would be more fitting: Personal Strait-Jacket.

"What are you musing about?"

She moved her gaze from the river bank on the other side of the bay to Scott's face to find him grinning at her.

"What? Something funny?"

"Not comfortable in that?" He reached over and unbuckled the top strap of her PFD. "We can adjust it."

"It's fine; I'll get used to it." She put her head on one side. "I can't rotate the paddle like you do. It rubs my hand, between my thumb and forefinger." She made an "O" to demonstrate. "Maybe gloves, do you think?"

"Whatever makes it easier. You'll be surprised at what a difference a few days can make." He reached over and ruffled her hair.

Georgie liked it when he did things like that. Simple affection.

She returned her gaze to the water. It had been nice, when she'd first pushed off from the shore, gliding along in the water—feeling the sun beating down on her shoulders and listening to the soft splash when her paddle bit into the water on either side, watching the fish and other people out in the bay. She hadn't been so keen on being tossed around by the bow wave when a fishing boat went by too fast, but now she knew to turn her nose into the wake; next time would be different.

"I like it," she said, feeling happy. "Will we be exploring many rivers?"

"Rivers, and lakes, and gorges. You'll see things that you can't see from land." Scott leaned back next to her, sharing the tree. "I'm looking forward to showing you Australia. So much to see."

"From the hinterland around Tamborine Mountain," Georgie said, "to the river and the sea here at Yamba. Both so different."

"Wait until you see the outback. Red dirt, blue sky. Great photos to send back home."

"They love the ones I've sent back already. No wonder your sisters want to live here."

"Hmm."

Naturally, her mention of his sisters turned their minds to the mysterious disappearance—and reappearance—of the portafilter.

"Lissa doesn't believe for one moment that she put it there behind the coffee mugs," Georgie said. "She said she *never* does. And I know I didn't, and Viv didn't."

"Plus the other things. The whisk, the measuring bowl."

"All back in strange places." Georgie stared unseeingly at the ripples on the water. "Not strange enough so you think instantly, *a break-in,* but enough so when you think about it, you say: "No, I would never have put it there. It's just *wrong.*"

They had all decided, earlier that day, that there was no other answer for it, but someone had gained access to the cafe during the night.

How, they didn't know. Nobody had been able to find any signs of a break-in.

But the big question was *why?* Why hide the portafilter, the other utensils?

It didn't make any sense. All it had done was create a nuisance for a day.

And, more importantly, alerted them to the fact that an enemy was getting closer and more daring.

"More daring," Georgie said aloud, "and more stupid."

Scott guessed what she was talking about. "Yes, stupid, because now we know for sure that someone is breaking in—so we won't let it happen again."

"Breaking in or *letting* themselves in," she said. "Stan Lambert probably has a key, remember. But surely he could just terminate the lease early if he wanted them out?"

"He'd have to pay out the lease if he did that. From what I hear, he loves making money, hates parting with it."

"He offered them a deal on the rent at the other complex," Georgie pointed out.

"Which, as we saw, is not in a good position for their business. Or anyone else. Four units, all empty at the moment."

Georgie thought about it. "What do we do? Fix an alarm? Stay there at night?"

"We could put in an alarm or a camera, but the girls can't afford too much."

"I could help out," Georgie offered.

"So could I. I've got savings, but they'll say no."

"And if they have to move to other premises, the money will be wasted."

"Mmm," he said, sounding frustrated. "I could try sleeping there for a few nights."

Georgie turned over a possibility in her mind. "You know what? I'm going to spend some time walking around town this afternoon. I'll chat to a few store owners, see if I can find out anything."

"About what?"

"About anything." She poked him in the ribs. "This detecting lark isn't a precise science, you know. I'm out looking for clues."

"Okay, Sherlock. While you're doing that, I'm going to have a chat with my brother. See if he's found out anything interesting about Stan Lambert yet."

"Good." Georgie stood up and brushed the sand off her legs. "It's about time we got the other members of the Crystal Ball Investigation Team onto this. Tonight, I'll call your mother: she can read the cards, and we'll see what we can come up with."

Cheered, she climbed back into the kayak, waited for Scott to move off, and followed him, studying his style again and trying to copy it.

One thing at a time, she thought, stroking through the water. Right now, it was all about kayaking. This afternoon, gossip with the townsfolk. Tonight, talk to the family astrologist and the family hacker about how they could find the bad guy. Then she could do another crystal ball reading.

Nobody could say she didn't lead a balanced life.

## 12

# The Grapevine

CHATTING TO STORE OWNERS, Georgie figured, would probably involve buying stuff, so she armed herself with a good-sized shopping bag before setting off up the street.

Sitting in a camp chair with his feet up on a folding footstool, Scott surveyed her with a grin. "Planning on picking up a few things?"

"I can't just go in and out asking questions. I'd look nosy, and people would talk."

"Why do I have a feeling that today might get expensive?"

"It could, yes. And then I'm going to torture you by unpacking everything and rearranging all the cupboards while I decide where to put it." Georgie checked that she had her purse and gave him a cheery wave. "I'm off to do some detecting."

"Good luck." Scott turned to the next page of his newspaper. "I'll sit here and catch up on the news of the world."

Georgie had a loose plan: talk to any business owner,

see where that led, and follow her nose. Half an hour later, she had bought a picture frame, a new tank top, and a cute leather-bound notebook. Which was all very nice, but she hadn't found out anything new. Mostly the conversation had run along the lines of: "You from America? Love your accent!" or "You're a friend of the girls at *Coffee, Cakes, and Crêpes*? Love their cupcakes!"

Finally, she had worked her way to the clothing store right next door to Viv's cafe. All along, this had been one of the places she was really interested in after learning from Viv's landlord that the owner was moving out.

*That* was suspicious. One person moving out, the other one getting *pushed* out?

The woman behind the counter looked up, and Georgie could tell from the slight change in her expression that she knew who had just walked in. Strange, Georgie thought, that Linda Malloy didn't ever pop in next door to grab a coffee or a crêpe for lunch. Lissa and Viv had shrugged and said that she didn't seem to socialize much with anyone, but she was also a friend of Stan Lambert's wife Yvonne, so that might have something to do with it.

"Hi," Georgie greeted her. She gestured towards the window display. "I like that turquoise top on the model. Do you have one in size six?"

Linda cast an assessing eye over Georgie. "American size six or Australian size six?"

"Oh. American. Sorry." Georgie tried to remember what that was in Australia but shrugged.

"That would be about a size 10. We have one, I'm sure." Linda came out from behind the counter and walked across to a circular clothing rack. Skimming through the hangers, she plucked out the turquoise top and held it out. "This should look nice with your coloring—and you know something else? It looks terrific with these slim-line white pants." She unhooked another hanger and held it out. "If you don't have any."

"Thanks. I'll try them both." Georgie headed for the change room, and a few minutes later, she was out again, opening her arms in a query. "Well?"

A genuinely appreciative smile appeared on Linda's face. "Yes. Perfect."

"I'll take them both." She disappeared again to change and then took the items to the cash register. "These are just what I need; I can wear them most places."

Linda caressed the silky fabric of the turquoise top. "I bought one of these myself, in a caramel shade."

"Lovely." Georgie decided to dive right in. "I was in the cafe next door when your landlord was visiting. He says you're going to move to the complex over near the mall—is that right? You won't miss being here in the township?" She nodded at the street outside, where there was a constant flow of people walking by.

Linda looked up sharply. "Stan told you that?"

*Oops,* thought Georgie. "He was suggesting alternative accommodation to Viv and Lissa, and he mentioned that you were moving across there. Thought it might be nice for them to have someone they know."

"I didn't know he'd done that." Linda concentrated on folding the clothes. "I haven't completely made up my mind."

"I'm Georgie, by the way, Scott's partner. Scott is Viv and Lissa's brother."

"I've seen him in there. You too." Linda rang up the

sale and handed back Georgie's credit card. "Nice to meet you, Georgie. So, uh, you're visiting for a while?"

"For a little while. Scott and I are traveling around Australia." Georgie settled in for a chat as though she'd known Linda for ten years rather than ten minutes. "This is our first stop so that we can spend some time with the family. Yamba is such a beautiful place. Have you lived here all your life?"

"No. I moved here to be with my husband, and we divorced," Linda said, her voice short. "I didn't see why I should move away when I liked living here, so I didn't; I just decided to use my maiden name again. I don't see him very often."

Georgie half-turned and let her eyes drift across the various displays. "You have good taste. I can see another half-dozen things I like already." She grinned at Linda.

"Well, don't let me stop you." Linda smiled back, unbending slightly.

"I might pop back tomorrow or the next day. I have to run a few errands for Viv right now. It's been so hard for them, with all the things that have gone wrong. One thing after another. It hardly seems fair." She gave a tiny frown and tilted her head at Linda. "You know about their run of bad luck, don't you? Yes, of course you do; you're right next door."

"I'd heard," Linda admitted cautiously. "Is, uh, everything all right now?"

Georgie sighed. "I *think* so. The wiring's okay, the water pipe's been fixed, and now they've been given a clean bill of health. It has shaken them a bit, though. They try to hide it, but I can tell. They're so *careful* about food storage, pests, all of that. It's really strange; they can't figure it out."

Linda fiddled with a jewelry display on the counter. "What do you mean?"

"Well…" Georgie let the silence stretch out while she looked searchingly at Linda. "I don't know how much I should say. I don't want to sound as though I'm the out-of-towner coming in and making waves."

Linda looked at her directly. "I don't gossip."

"No! Goodness! I didn't mean to imply you were." She decided to be upfront. "But I heard you're a good friend of Stan's wife, Yvonne. And Scott's sisters have enough problems—I don't want anything I say to create more tension between them and their landlord."

Linda shrugged. "I met Yvonne when I was married to Ron; he and Stan are friends. I still see her occasionally, but not as much."

Georgie's ears pricked up. Ron someone, a friend of Stan Lambert's…something else to chase up. Meanwhile, she might as well keep talking, see what came out of it. She wasn't getting any negative feelings from Linda Malloy.

*Plunge in, Georgie.*

"The thing is…Viv and Lissa can't help wondering if someone might want them out. *Some* of the things that have happened might have happened to anyone, but all of them?" Georgie shook her head. "Those cockroaches. Rotting food. It just didn't make sense. They're jittery."

Linda said nothing, but a lot was going on behind her eyes.

Georgie leaned forward a tiny bit more, making her eyes large and earnest. "And that rotting food was *fish*."

"Oh, yes?" Linda clearly didn't understand the significance.

"They don't serve fish. They have never cooked fish or seafood in there. So…*fish?*"

"Oh." Linda looked to one side, thinking, and then out at the people walking by. "That does seem odd."

"Yes. That's what they thought."

Georgie decided she had gone far enough. She'd planted a few seeds. "Anyway, I've got to run." She patted her shopping bag and beamed. "A successful morning's shopping!"

She left, knowing she'd given Linda something to think about. And who knew what else might come out of it? It was a risk if Linda talked to the wrong person—but sometimes you had to shake a few trees.

13

# Crystal Ball Again

Late that afternoon, Scott pressed fresh snapper fillets from the Fishermen's Co-Op into seasoned breadcrumbs and then seared them lightly, while Georgie tossed salad greens with avocado and pine nuts. She found some light classical music on their playlist, Scott poured crisp white wine, and they sat down to eat.

Georgie met his eyes and smiled while they clinked glasses. "Life's good."

"It is indeed." Scott took a bite and nodded with a sigh of appreciation. "Can't beat good, simple food. Crusted snapper, salad, and wine."

They ate outside, talking about kayaking and their trip and the surrounding Clarence River valley, keeping it light and easy while responding to greetings from other campers who walked past their site. The late summer evening was warm, with a pleasant breeze from Yamba Bay, and they could hear laughter and chat outside RVs all along the waterfront. The sun sank over the horizon, and they stayed outside until the bright colors of sunset faded to the purple of dusk.

"Well." Finally, Scott stirred. "Time to clean up and then see what the crystal ball has to tell us?"

"And put in a call to your mom." Georgie stood up and collected their plates. "I know your sisters don't want to worry her, but she knows something's up. She'll be waiting to hear from us."

"They still haven't said anything to her?" Scott grimaced as he picked up their glasses and followed her into their caravan. "That'll go down well. Mum's not one to sit on the sidelines if her chicks are under threat."

"They said they were going to call her this afternoon. I asked them to do it before supper, so she could look at the cards before I called tonight."

"Does she know you'll be in touch?"

"I sent her a text."

Efficiently, they cleaned up, already in a comfortable rhythm, moving around the caravan together. Just before eight, Georgie switched on an LED candle that gave her the soft flickering light she wanted without the risk of the smoke alarm shrieking.

Scott watched while she set the crystal ball between them and slid off the black velvet cloth that she used to cover it. The candlelight added depth and warmth to the crystal ball, and Georgie suddenly had a good feeling about tonight.

She was going to find out something.

She glanced up at Scott, who nodded.

"You feel it too?" she asked.

"I feel *something*. Confidence, maybe."

Georgie sat back and let the anticipation grow.

Outside, she could still hear the soft murmur of voices from a small group outside an RV a few sites away and the muted sound of a TV nearby. Then everything faded, and as she rested her fingertips on the crystal, she felt the hard surface grow warmer under her touch.

In the center of the globe, a soft pearly mist began to form. Georgie watched and let herself be drawn into the drifting tendrils while an image formed.

An old woman appeared, her dark eyes snapping with life and her wrinkled face stretching in a smile.

*Rosa.*

Georgie felt her lips curve in an answering smile as she stared at her great-grandmother's image, and when she glanced up at Scott, she saw that he was grinning too.

"I wondered how long it would be before she paid a visit," he said. "Her only great-granddaughter on the other side of the world and all, with *her* crystal ball. She had to turn up sooner or later."

"*My* crystal ball now," Georgie reminded him, although she knew that it would always be partly Rosa's. Just as she was certain that the globe itself probably held an imprint of those before Rosa who had had the Sight.

*Hello, Rosa,* she thought and then focused on holding an image of Viv and Lissa in her mind. There was no doubt in her mind that Rosa already knew there was trouble. Now it remained to be seen whether she could help out…from eight and a half thousand miles away.

In the crystal ball, Rosa's face turned until she was in profile, and her eyes narrowed as though she was watching something. Or someone.

Then her image dissolved, and in its place, Scott's mother appeared, staring down at something out of sight. Georgie could guess what she was looking at: she'd seen that look on Louise's face before when she was studying the cards laid out before her.

A moment later, it was confirmed: Georgie and Scott could see her hands moving quickly, dealing cards, before the movement stopped.

Then they, too, were looking at the cards.

"An astrological spread," Scott murmured, leaning forward and looking intently at the tiny image in the crystal ball.

"So Rosa's telling us to listen to Louise? I would have anyway."

Then Louise and the cards disappeared. Georgie waited, certain there was more.

Rosa appeared again, for just a blink of an eye, and then, very slowly, another image formed. Georgie frowned and tried to make sense of what she was seeing.

A group of women.

Women? She'd had a growing certainty that it was a man—or men—behind the chain of events at *Coffee, Cakes & Crepes*, but she'd been wrong before.

Hiding the portafilter on the coffee machine, hiding other things—that seemed petty, just something to make life harder. Scott had commented that it felt like the work of a woman, but Georgie wasn't so sure.

The women in the crystal ball were all sitting in a circle, passing something around. Georgie squinted, trying to see what it was, but then abruptly, she wasn't looking at the whole group but at a pair of hands, holding an object.

"It's a square from a quilt!" she exclaimed, looking at the careful stitching around the picture formed from colorful scraps of fabric and the rough edges that showed the batting in the center.

The square was passed from hand to hand, and then the image dissolved completely.

A glance at Scott showed that he was as puzzled as she was. "That picture in the square," he said. "What was it? Anything significant?"

Without taking her eyes from the crystal ball, Georgie tried to remember. "It looked like a bunch of flowers. Don't know what that means." She held up a hand for silence, watching intently. Something else was appearing in the mist, but it was indistinct.

A blocky-looking building with a table out front. Two-story…was that a flash of orange? Georgie peered closer, but it was already fading.

She could feel the warmth of the crystal ball fading under her fingertips, and sure enough, the mist gradually dissipated.

Feeling somewhat disappointed, she sat back and huffed out a sigh. "It's gone. I thought I'd get more than that."

"It must mean something," Scott said mildly, patting her hand. "Let's think. It all has to add up to something."

"All right." Georgie sat back. "First, we saw Rosa."

"Which means something in itself," Scott pointed out. "Every time she's appeared in the past, it's been a signal to pay attention."

"Especially in my first attempts," Georgie said wryly, thinking back to her early days experimenting with the crystal ball, completely unsure of what she should be doing.

"The second image was mum," Scott said, "and she

will have done several spreads after the girls' phone call. Ask her about the astrological one."

Feeling more cheered, Georgie nodded. "Okay. Then, after Louise, we saw the women with the quilt square."

"Featuring a basket of flowers." Scott made a face. "The actual design may or may not be significant. It could be more a push for you to—"

"Find the group of women," Georgie finished for him. "Yes, I thought of that. Adele has a quilting group —she's the woman I met at the bakery. I was planning on turning up one day anyway to tell them about my quilt, and do some work on the square from Tamborine Mountain."

"When do they meet?"

"Not sure. I can find out." Georgie's mind moved to the final image. "And finally a building. This case seems to be all about buildings and landlords...I wonder if this is another building owned by Stan Lambert? Maybe someone else is having trouble with him?"

"I didn't recognize it." Scott's brow furrowed in the same way as Georgie's when she tried to recall an image. "It was there and gone in the blink of an eye, and it was fuzzy anyway."

"I saw a flash of orange, and a table. With an umbrella."

"Yes, I caught that. We could drive around, look for something similar. Yamba's not that big."

"All right. We'll put it on the to-do list."

Scott sat back. "You didn't get any impressions, sudden thoughts about any of this?"

"Not today," Georgie admitted regretfully. "Not a

whisper. Images only. This can be *such* a frustrating game."

She took a last look at the crystal ball, but it was completely clear, winking back at her in the flickering light of the candle. "All right. How about you write down what you remember, and I'll phone your mum."

Louise, and an astrological spread…

Suddenly, deep inside her, she felt a flicker of hope.

They *could* solve this.

Just as long as nothing too bad happened to Viv and Lissa while they were going through the process.

# 14

# Calling Louise

From the speed with which Louise answered the call, Georgie guessed that she had probably been sitting there waiting.

"Georgie? Thank goodness. I've been dying to compare notes with you," Louise said immediately, her voice loud and clear through the phone's speaker. "Oh, I'm sorry, that was rude. How are you enjoying Yamba?"

Georgie and Scott both laughed.

"We are having a great time, thanks, Louise," Georgie said, "but I can understand you've got a bit on your mind at the moment. You've heard from Viv and Lissa?"

"Yes, a couple of hours ago." A note of censure entered into Louise's normally cheerful tone. "I can't believe those girls waited this long before telling me what's been going on. Smack on the hand for those two."

"I think they were hoping it was just a run of bad

luck, that they would sort themselves out." Georgie met Scott's eyes and bit back a smile as he slashed a finger across his throat.

"Well, it's not as though I'm some decrepit old bat that has to be protected from all this," Louise went on in an aggrieved tone. "They know that I can help if I have the facts."

Scott opened both hands out to the side, and mouthed "*See?*"

Moving on quickly, Georgie said, "I'm sure you've done a reading tonight. I've just finished doing one here, with the crystal ball. The first thing I saw was Rosa, and immediately after that, an image of you reading the cards. I wasn't sure whether that was about tonight or whether you were already picking up on something."

"I love the way your great-grandmother pops in to say hello," Louise exclaimed in true delight. "I *wish* that I could do what you do. I wonder if I could learn?"

Georgie thought of how Louise interpreted both cards and horoscopes in such an intuitive way and immediately nodded. "I'm sure you could. You're already tapping into something." She looked at Scott and laughed. "Your son is nodding here in agreement."

"Mind you," Scott put in, leaning close to the phone and raising his voice, "you don't *need* Rosa to appear in a crystal ball. You already talk to her more often than she talks to her own family."

"She's fantastic. I wish she lived closer." Then Louise's voice became more businesslike. "But let's talk about the girls. We had a long talk this afternoon, and I think they've told me everything—from when things started to go wrong, with the rewiring expenses, the broken pipe, that ridiculous situation with being asked to move tables on Melbourne Cup day—can you *believe* that?—and then having to close down because of those flaming cockroaches. *Cockroaches*." Anger made her voice rise a few decibels.

"What's your take on all this?"

"Oh, they're being targeted. No doubt at all."

"Sabotage?"

"Absolutely. I can't tell you how glad I am that you and Scotty are there to give them some support. I suggested to Tony that we come down too, but he said no. What do you think?"

Georgie looked at Scott. He shook his head.

"Maybe not just yet. Give it a couple more days, see what we can find out."

"All right," Louise said, her voice resigned. "That seems to be the consensus, then. Now, do you want to go first, or shall I?"

"I'll tell you what I saw, first."

"Fine. Fire away."

For the next five minutes, Georgie sketched a quick picture of what had happened since they arrived in Yamba—finding the cafe closed, doing a reading, and getting the impression that there was more than one person involved, and the different personalities of the people she'd met. She finished off with a quick rundown of what she had seen in the crystal ball.

"That's about it, I think." She looked at Scott. "Did I leave out anything?"

"Only that I've also put in a call to Bluey, but I haven't heard back yet. He's checking into Stan Lambert for us, and anyone who might be in business with him. See if there's anything in his background."

"Good," said Louise. "One way or the other, we'll get to the bottom of this. All right, let me tell you what I've seen in the cards. I've been doing a few different spreads, and, as Georgie saw, one of the ones that made me take a second look was the astrological spread. There's somebody significant that you should be looking at. It's a female, an Aries. She is amenable, caring, but that's led her into trouble. And aligned with her in some way, I see another female—someone a bit more intense, determined, who has been somewhat impatient with the first one. This one is older and either a Taurus or a Gemini. I'm leaning towards Taurus."

Georgie was scribbling on a notepad and pen that she had in readiness. "Okay, got it. Co-operative Aries, linked with an older woman, Taurus or Gemini. So the older one might be more of a community leader, perhaps?" She thought of Irene Wilson, with a finger in every pie. She'd have to check and see what birth sign she was. "This first one, the Aries. Are you getting a sense that she is the sort of person who is always helping out in the community, or that she is easily led and pushed around?"

Louise hesitated for a moment and then said slowly, "Maybe people presume upon her good nature? Look for women's groups; she might be one of those worker bees who turn up all the time and rarely get any of the accolades."

"Hmmm." Georgie's mind went immediately to the group of women she had seen with the quilting square. "Would this be connected with the quilting group I saw?"

"Could be." Louise's voice sharpened with interest.

"If you relate your reading to mine, then that might be where you'd find her."

"Okay. What else?"

"You said you had a feeling that there were men involved. And more than one?"

"Gut feeling." Georgie laughed. "Don't ask me to explain."

"Wouldn't dream of it. I think you're right. I see two men involved, with a third kind of on the periphery. When I link it with Viv and Lissa, that is. The one to watch is Cancer, but I think on the cusp, so it could be a Leo. Look for someone with a birthday in late July, early August. The other one, I'm getting a sense it's a Capricorn."

Georgie nodded as she scribbled. "I can see I'm going to have a challenge in front of me, finding out when everyone's birthday is."

"Could be awkward," Louise admitted. "With me, it's not a problem. Everyone expects an astrologer to be curious about birthdays."

Scott raised a hand.

Georgie grinned at him. "You may speak."

"Just an idea," Scott suggested. "Maybe Viv and Lissa could collect birthdays, tell everyone they get a free cup of coffee on their special day. And a cupcake with a candle in it."

Georgie regarded him with awe. "You know, that's a really good idea."

"I have them occasionally," he said modestly.

"There's something else," Louise went on. "They said they had a broken water pipe a few months back, and it caused problems?"

"That's right."

"Tell them to look at that again. Or maybe check the roof for leaks. I see further problems with water."

"Right."

"And suggest they check their house, too," Louise added as an afterthought. "I saw water, but it doesn't necessarily have to be the cafe. *And* it could be storm damage. Pay attention to the weather report: there's some nasty weather coming your way."

"All right, I'll tell them." Georgie looked at her scribbled notes. "Anything else?"

"Not right now, but now that I know what's going on, there could be. I'll keep doing readings. Meanwhile, I have a strong feeling about this group of women, especially the two that I mentioned. Follow that up, if you can."

"I will. I'll ask Adele when the quilting group meets —I wanted to go there anyway, to do my first square. And I want to show them the quilt you made for me, so they can see how I got inspired."

"I wish I could be there with you. Now, you will keep me informed, won't you, Georgie? Even if those naughty girls tell you not to worry me?"

"I promise," Georgie said, meaning every word. "It's worse not to know. And anyway, you're part of the investigation team now, remember?"

"So I am." Louise sounded happier. "I'll call you if I pick up anything else."

She rang off, and Georgie sat back, going over everything she'd shared with Louise, before looking at Scott. "What do you think? Did anything stand out for you?"

"Mainly," he said wryly, "that Viv and Lissa are in trouble. But they've got us, as Mum said. And whoever is messing with them is going to find it's a lot harder now." He looked uncharacteristically grim.

Georgie reached over and took his hand. "They're family, Scott. I don't like seeing *anyone* treated badly... but family? They'll regret it."

---

15

# Maureen's Rebellion

---

MAUREEN WATCHED Trevor Chaffey's white Ute come to a stop outside *Coffee, Cakes & Crepes*, just as it did every morning. When the cafe had closed down for a few days, he'd called in once to get a cappuccino from her instead, but she could tell by the expression on his face while he watched her make it that she was doing something wrong.

He'd paid for it and not said a word, polite as always, but he'd never asked for another one. Fish and chips, yes, but no coffee.

The driver's door opened, and Trev got out, walking around the back of the Ute to check that the ladder was secure on its racks above the shining checker plate toolboxes and that all straps were tight. He had a reputation around town as a good, reliable tradesman. Trev always turned up when he said he would, did more than needed, and charged reasonable fees.

There'd been a whisper or two around town that he was keen on Viv Mowbray, but she'd never seen them out together.

In ten minutes, Trev was out again, and shortly after that, young Amber Kaye pulled up in Shane Carter's white van from the bakery. Amber always wore white—her idea of what an apprentice should wear, Maureen thought—but it was inevitably close-fitting and low-cut.

Amber Kaye, in Maureen's humble opinion, was little more than a tramp, and Shane Carter had rocks in his head for dropping Viv to take up with Amber.

There were, she reflected, a lot of men who wouldn't be able to see a good thing if it came up and bit them.

*That* thought had her turning around to look at her husband, Jim.

Forty-seven years, she'd been married to Jim Beggs. Doing his bidding, helping him run the cafe, maintaining his house, and listening to his never-ending grumbling.

Having to justify every penny she spent.

Jim turned to get the batter out of the fridge and caught her watching him. Immediately, his mouth turned down at the corners and his eyebrows lowered. "If you've got nothing better to do, you might get yourself out here and lend a hand. I've got that backpacker coming in soon to show him the ropes." His voice was heavy with resentment, implying that he wouldn't *need* to hire a backpacker if she pulled her weight.

His words made her see red. *If you have nothing better to do.* She had a *hundred* things she'd rather do. It was all right for Jim to go AWOL several times a week playing golf with his mates, but when she wanted a morning off to join Adele's quilting group or learn photography with Chris, that was a different kettle of fish.

Jim pointed at the chopping board and the iceberg lettuce waiting on it. "Lettuce needs shredding."

And that was another thing: Jim didn't hold with what he termed new-fangled machines that might lighten the load a bit. He wouldn't know what *julienne* meant, and he wouldn't care.

*No*, thought Maureen. *Shred the lettuce yourself.*

Followed by, with a new, burning resentment: *I really don't like you, Jim Beggs.*

Grumpy old sod could handle it himself for half an hour. It wasn't as though they were overrun with customers.

Maureen turned her back on him, untied her apron, folded it tidily, and tucked it under the counter. She grabbed her purse, lifted the counter flap, let it bang down behind her, and walked out of the door, ignoring his furious "Maureen! Where the hell are you going?" as she went down the steps and across the road and into *Coffee, Cakes & Crepes* where the women were nice to her and where they had the best cupcakes she had ever tasted.

Behind the coffee machine, Lissa glanced up to see who was coming in. Amber, swinging an empty tray, came out of the kitchen with a stony-faced Viv following her and stopped abruptly.

Georgie stopped inserting napkins in the silver holders, poised with a stack in one hand.

They all stared at her.

Heaven knew what they could see on her face.

"Lissa," she said, "could I have a cappuccino, please? In a mug. Low-fat milk. And..." she glanced at the display cabinet, where she could see cupcakes with mocha-colored swirls of icing and chocolate flakes. "And one of those chocolate cupcakes. Thanks."

She marched over to the coffee table that held a neat

stack of magazines, picked one up, and made herself comfortable on the big squishy dusky pink sofa that she'd never had time to sit on before.

For a moment, there was dead silence in the room. Maureen buried her head in the magazine, flipping pages without seeing anything, almost in a panic at her daring, and of course, it was Amber who spoke first.

"Are you all right, Maureen?" Her voice held speculation rather than concern. "Your Jim's standing over there on the steps with his hands on his hips looking like he's ready to kill someone."

"I'm fine, thank you, Amber."

Viv's voice cut in. "See you later, Amber. Georgie will run your order down later. Nine-thirty, right?"

"I'll take them now. I'll wait."

"Not right now. Nine thirty." Viv's voice brooked no argument.

"Well, *fine.*"

She heard the sound of footsteps walking out, and the door closed.

Maureen felt the cushion beside her dip, and a slim hand closed over hers, stopping her from turning more pages. She looked up, and it was Lissa, looking at her with compassion. "Are you really all right, Maureen?"

Feeling as though she was in some alternate reality, inhabiting the body of a different Maureen Beggs, she nodded. "I just needed a break. Don't worry; he won't come over here." She glanced back to their cafe across the road and was suddenly struck with how shabby and unwelcoming it looked. No wonder the locals were starting to go to places like this.

Places filled with light and friendly faces. Places

where you could get nice coffee and cupcakes baked by Viv.

Jim, apparently done with giving *Coffee, Cakes & Crepes* the stink eye, turned on his heel and slammed his way back inside.

Maureen put the magazine down.

"Lissa," she said, "Can I watch you make that coffee? See what I'm doing wrong? I know I'm coming to your class on Sunday, but—"

Lissa smiled, her warm light brown eyes kind under the bright orange hair that Jim hated so much. "Of course you can. Come on. I'll make your coffee, and you drink it and take a few moments for yourself. And Maureen? Any time we're not busy, I'm happy to show you. You don't have to wait for a class."

Maureen got up. "Thank you." Turning her back to the window and the shop where she'd spent far too much of her life, she followed Lissa and watched carefully while she prepared the coffee and the milk, explaining every step.

And then the door opened again, and she heard Irene Wilson's gasp before she said in amazement, "Maureen Beggs? What are *you* doing over here?"

Jim would be watching, for sure, knowing that the town's biggest gossip had seen his wife go over to the opposition.

He'd be livid, and Maureen was *glad*.

She'd have to go back over there soon, but it was so good to have a break.

"Hello, Irene," she said, hoping her smile was convincing. "I've been meaning to ask you—which morning does Adele's quilting group meet?"

Over the road, Jim savagely chopped at the lettuce and swept it into a bowl. What in tarnation had come over Maureen, he couldn't begin to imagine. She *knew* he had a new backpacker to train, and she was the one who usually showed them the ropes while he got on with things.

She'd better get herself back on over here fast, or there'd be the devil to pay. Ever since those Mowbray women had opened the cafe, things had gone downhill. His regulars were still happy enough with a pot of tea or coffee from the old percolator, but now the tourists all wanted cappuccino and latte and other things he didn't know the name of, and Maureen was the only one who knew how to make them.

Not that she seemed to be very good at it.

Despite himself, he kept going to the doorway between the kitchen and the cafe and looking at *Coffee, Cakes & Crepes*. Already, two retirees from the caravan park were sitting outside, watching the early morning street traffic while they waited for their order.

Stupid idea, tables out on the footpath. Why would you want to sit outside when there was perfectly good seating inside? Maureen could carry on all she liked; he wasn't going to give in on that one.

Behind the tourists, sitting inside on the other side of the window, he could see Irene Wilson and Janet Cox gossiping away as usual while they drank coffee and ate cake. No wonder Irene was the size of a house.

He squinted but couldn't see Maureen. Was she still in there? If she was, he'd be willing to bet that Irene would be across here on some flimsy excuse to rub it in.

He fumed for another ten minutes until finally, someone walked up the steps and into his cafe—someone young, tanned, with a ready grin and a cocky walk. The backpacker who'd called in yesterday to see about work, saying he'd met a guy who used to work here, said it was worth coming in to ask.

Jim couldn't remember his name.

"So, you're here." He jerked his head in the direction of the kitchen. "Hope you're a fast learner."

"Don't worry, I am," the kid said.

"What was your name again?"

"Anton. Remember, I told you that I met someone who worked for you?"

Jim grunted. He'd had so many casual workers over the years; it could have been any one of dozens.

"Nick," Anton said, watching him as though the name should mean something. "Nick *Egan*. Met him down at Woolgoolga last week."

*Nick Egan.* Okay, he knew who that was; his memory wasn't that bad. Nick had been with them for two months. He'd worked out all right until a couple of weeks ago when he'd said it was time to leave.

Leaving him in the lurch, as they all did.

Still, he'd certainly had his uses.

"All right, yeah, I remember." Jim looked at the messy kitchen and then at the coffee machine. "You said you can cook fish and chips, make hamburgers, make fancy coffee, clean up. Right?"

"Right."

"Wife's not here to run you through it. Can you handle it?"

Anton gave him a pitying grin, cocky as all hell. "Yeah, man. What do you want me to do first?"

Behind him, Jim saw Irene and Janet leave *Coffee, Cakes & Crepes* and step off the footpath, heading in his direction.

"See those two women crossing the road?" he said. "I can't stand a bar of either one. You serve them; tell them I'm busy."

He grabbed Maureen's apron, tossed it at the kid, and went to hide.

When Maureen came back, she was going to cop the sharp edge of his tongue. After that, she and the new kid could run the place while he met up with his mates for a round of golf.

She had some bee in her bonnet, and he just didn't have the patience for this kind of nonsense.

# 16

# Teeing Off

STAN LAMBERT DID a lot of wheeling and dealing on the golf course. Any way you cut it, the Yamba Country Club had done a lot to line his pockets over the years.

He reserved one Friday afternoon a month to schmooze with three of the local yokels. They convened at around 1 o'clock: nine holes in winter, eighteen in summer, and then conducted business in the club afterward.

Right now, he was waiting for Jim Beggs to show up while he and the local dentist talked to Ron Foley about offering incentives to his ex-wife to move out of her shop. The developer who'd approached Stan was ready to buy the premises *now*, but Linda was stalling. After being married to Ron for two years, she sensed there was something in the wind. Probably digging her toes in until Stan paid out her lease, and *that* wasn't going to happen any time soon.

He hadn't accumulated wealth by throwing money away.

Between the four of them, they had some profitable

investments in Yamba and surrounding towns. Jim's dull wife Maureen had no clue that her husband, slaving away selling fish and chips every day, was worth nearly two million dollars.

After grooming the four men for years, Stan knew how to play them. Jim Beggs and Ron Foley had gone to school together, played football together, and got into trouble together. They'd both done it tough in the early years before climbing onto the property bandwagon. Ron was a bullet-headed, hard man who still wasn't opposed to interpreting the law in creative ways. He could be a bully and was open to a bit of trickery, which was useful to Stan because he liked to keep his reputation squeaky clean.

Stephen Patterson was a bloodhound when it came to sniffing out a good deal, which was somewhat surprising, seeing he spent his days in a dental surgery staring into people's mouths. Being married to Kerry probably helped: she was one of those people on every committee going.

As for Jim: he had his cronies who came in most days to his old-fashioned fish and chip shop, and those cronies had cronies. Jim had brought just as much to the table as the other two, but the only investment that his wife knew about was the modest duplex over near the mall.

"Here's Jim now," Ron said. "Unusual for him to be late."

They watched Jim approach, and it was clear by the way he stalked across from the clubhouse that he was not a happy man.

"Uh oh," Ron said. "What's old Maureen done this time?"

"Made him drink her attempts at fancy coffee, probably," Stephen said, and they all laughed.

Jim's frown deepened when he reached them, his eyes moving from one face to another. "What?" he demanded truculently, heaving his golf clubs onto the cart.

"You're late," Ron said, needling him. "That means an extra round of drinks after the game."

"New backpacker," Jim said shortly. "Are we going to get this moving or not?"

Stan exchanged a swift glance with Stephen. When Jim was in a mood, he was in a mood. The best chance to get him out of it was to dangle money in front of him.

"Forget the new backpacker, Jimbo," he said. "They're a dime a dozen. Think "new investment opportunity"."

Jim grunted.

"What's got your knickers in a twist?" Unfazed by Jim's bad temper, Ron elbowed him. "Why don't you hire somebody decent? You can afford it."

"Maureen doesn't know that," Jim said. "And I don't want her to know." He pulled out a driver. "My turn to play with Stan. You tossed a coin yet?"

"Yes," Stan said. "We tee off first. You go ahead."

With another grunt, Jim pulled on his gloves and bent down to put the tee on the marker. They all watched while he shuffled a bit, wiggled his hips, and finally took the shot.

The ball veered off to the left, and Jim swished his driver through the air, looking even grimmer.

"Gonna take him the whole eighteen to cool down," muttered Ron.

Stan waved that off. "He'll be cool once we tell him the profits we stand to make."

"Maybe so," Ron said, "but we're all over-extended. We need to move things along."

"You do your share," Stan said, "and I'll do mine. Talk to Linda, do whatever's necessary to bring things to a head."

"I will; I will." Ron nodded at the tee. "Go on. Make it good."

"Just make sure *you* lose; keep him happy."

Stan picked up his driver. He'd rather be anywhere else but on the golf course with Jim in one of his moods, but the man had money to burn.

He also owned a valuable piece of real estate smack in the middle of Yamba that Stan had his eye on, and once he finally got tired of cooking fish and chips, he might be persuaded to sell it.

That old shop, plus the real estate either side and behind that Stan owned, could be parlayed into a pot of gold. And as of now, Jim had no idea that Stan was the well-camouflaged new owner of the shoe store next door.

Today, he needed to make sure they had a win to get the cranky old devil into a decent frame of mind.

He set about playing his best game.

---

Back at Jim Beggs' cafe, his wife Maureen felt more mellow than she had for months.

Maybe *years*.

She had stayed in *Coffee, Cakes & Crepes* that morning for a good hour, drinking coffee until she buzzed and sampling Viv's cupcakes and talking to that nice Georgie woman from America.

She felt *normal*. If this was what retirement felt like, she was determined to get some of it for herself. If Jim wanted to work himself into the ground to save a dollar, let him.

In two more months, she would be sixty-five, and she wasn't working a day beyond that. She didn't care if they were poor—and why would they be when they had that nice little duplex over in Kingfisher Avenue and their house? They could live off the rent from the duplex and sell the cafe. The land must be worth a bit, even if the building was old and in need of repair…and she did have her mother's money, although the will had stipulated that Jim wasn't to see a red cent.

He'd be furious—more than furious.

Naturally, Irene Wilson had been agog to find out what was going on the minute she walked in and saw Maureen in enemy territory. When Maureen refused to say why she was at *Coffee, Cakes & Crepes* and not at work, Irene had dragged Janet across the road at the first opportunity to 'put in an order for lunch', as though anyone couldn't see through that.

She'd been back in ten minutes, none the wiser, after Jim had fobbed her off with the new backpacker kid.

When Maureen finally returned to work, her husband turned his back on her and didn't speak a word right up until the time he stomped out of the door to go and play golf, leaving her with their new recruit.

Right now, the backpacker was efficiently making cappuccinos for a couple of tourists. Maureen looked at him thoughtfully. Now that she'd committed to Adele's quilting group, she needed to organize Monday mornings.

"Anton?"

He turned and flashed a wide smile. "Yep?"

"How long are you planning to stay in Yamba?"

He shrugged. "A few months, maybe? I need to save some money before I travel again."

Maureen beamed at him. A few months, perfect. After that, she'd be retired and past caring what Jim did with the cafe.

"Can you work every Monday morning? Say, eight through until midday?"

"Sure."

Maureen thought about it for another thirty seconds and hastily revised the time frame. "No, let's say until one-thirty." One thirty would give her a chance to have lunch with the women in the group.

"Whatever." He expertly jiggled the milk jug, making a pretty design on the top of the coffee.

How did people *do* that? Lissa had tried to show her, but she had messed up.

Well, she had a barista class coming up on Sunday. Only now, she wasn't going to hide it from Jim.

It was liberating, not caring what he thought or said anymore.

And if he did carry on? Well, she'd just keep her mother's money and go and start again.

And be *happy*.

# 17

# Go Team!

THE NEXT DAY, after an uncomfortable night sleeping on a camp stretcher at *Coffee, Cakes & Crêpes*, and hearing nothing but a dog barking a few doors down, Scott decided to work out a few of the kinks by joining the surfers at the Angourie surf break just down the road. Georgie was helping out at the cafe while Lissa was running a course in Grafton, so it was the perfect opportunity.

When he returned to the car and checked his phone, he found a message to call his brother.

"Hey, bro," he said when Jeff picked up. "What's new?"

"I rang Georgie," Jeff said in an aggrieved tone, "and she said you were surfing. *Surfing.* And I'm stuck here in an office with no windows."

Scott grinned. "Surf's pumping here at Angourie. Pity you're not here."

Jeff groaned. "You're at Angourie? That's too cruel."

"We just bought new kayaks, too," Scott said,

rubbing it in. "Probably go for a paddle along the Esk later today."

"Sounds like you're too busy to investigate crime. Forget it. Have a nice day." The phone went dead.

Scott laughed, put his phone on the front seat, and stowed his surfboard in the car. A minute later, the phone rang again.

"I can't help it," Jeff said with a martyred sigh. "I can't let the bad guys get away with it."

"What have you got?"

"First, the landlord. Stan Lambert. When you said he owns half of Yamba, you weren't kidding. He's one of those people who have corporations hiding in corporations hiding in corporations. It's going to take me more than one session to dig deeper."

Scott nodded, gazing out across the ocean at the surfers waiting for the next wave. He thought of Georgie saying; there's *more than one person involved*. "We need to see what he's got going with other people in the town. Georgie's picked up a bit through local gossip; the man's always on the golf course with someone or other. He's tied up with various local Council groups as well. You could look at the wife, Yvonne: she's a bit of a mover and shaker too."

"Okay. He's got some investments with Jim Beggs, I see. And there's another guy you might want to take a closer look at, name of Ron Foley."

"Ron Foley? Georgie mentioned a Ron somebody. I'll ask the girls about him. But why?"

"He's been the subject of legal action a couple of times, and there's been a question of bribes. It looks like he's one of those blokes who like to take shortcuts. Intimidation, too."

"That would fit with someone who'd break in and make mischief." Scott deliberated over the information for a few seconds. "But hiding part of a coffee machine for a night? Would he do that?"

"If not him, then who? Why would *anyone* do that?"

"To make the girls doubt themselves," Scott said, thinking aloud. "Have them wondering if they'd really lost it or just misplaced it. Foley? I don't know: he doesn't sound the subtle type. More likely to break in and vandalize something."

He leaned on the car, watching one of the surfers catch a wave while he mentally ran through the women whose names had come up. Amber Kaye from the bakery, Linda Malloy in the shop next door, Irene Wilson the town gossip, and Maureen Beggs, who had surprised everyone the day before by leaving Jim fuming across the road while she had a coffee at his sisters' place. Would any of them break in?

He couldn't see it.

Stan Lambert's wife, Yvonne…would she? He didn't know much about her.

"You still there?" came Bluey's voice in his ear.

"Yeah. Just thinking. I'll send you a list of women's names, just to see if anything comes up."

"Right. For what it's worth, if this isn't about petty revenge, you should follow the money. With the kind of guys you're looking at, it's always about money—or power." Jeff's voice grew fainter on the last word, and Scott could hear him talking to someone. When he came back, he sounded distracted. "I have to go; I need to do some work for my *real* job. Send a text if you want me to look at anyone else."

"Okay. Thanks. Oh, wait, one more thing…can you send me everyone's date of birth?"

Bluey chuckled. "I see our mother's hand in this. All right, but I'm not finding out the exact hour and minute they arrived on this earth, so don't ask."

"Would I do that?"

"I've seen you reading those cards, bro. You and Ma are tarred with the same brush. See you, gotta run."

Scott tossed his towel in on top of the surfboard and got behind the wheel, thinking about what Bluey had found.

Someone who liked to take shortcuts and wasn't averse to a bit of intimidation? It might indeed be worth looking harder.

Ron Foley pushed open the door of his ex-wife's clothing store and strolled in. Linda was busy at the back, looking into one of the change rooms and talking to whoever was in there.

"You know, I think I liked this one on you better," she told the invisible customer. "Those splashes of cobalt and scarlet really pop. And weren't you saying you had too much black in your wardrobe?"

A woman's voice said, "But don't those bright colors make me look bigger?"

"Rather the opposite, I think," Linda said. "They draw the eye; the focus is on the pattern, not what's underneath it." She gave a light laugh. "Anyway, Chris, you're not overweight. I don't know why you're worried about it."

"I do like the colors."

"And you came in here determined to buy anything *but* black, right?"

"Right. Okay, I'll take those two tops and the light-weight cream pants."

"Good decision."

He saw a hand emerge from behind the curtain, passing two more items to Linda, who turned around and immediately scowled when she saw him. She said nothing until she got closer and then said in an undertone, "What are you doing here?"

Ron smiled at her cheerfully. If there was one thing he was good at, it was knowing how to get under Linda's skin. Remaining upbeat when she was hissing at him would do the trick every time.

"Linda, honey. No need to be like that." He kept his voice low, inclining his head at the change rooms. "No need to let everyone know our business, either."

Linda snorted. "As if everyone in Yamba doesn't *already* know our business. You didn't exactly hide it when you were chatting up backpackers or bedding the barmaid at the pub."

"I believe "bar attendant" is the correct terminology these days." He held up a hand and pretended to wince as she opened her mouth, ready to fire back at him. "Okay, bad joke, I know."

"Only you would consider that to be a joke." She cast a glance towards the back of the shop. "If you're not here to buy something, then go."

"If you agree to meet me for a cup of coffee."

She rolled her eyes. "I don't think so."

"A drink, then. Over at the club. We need to talk."

Linda stopped folding up the clothes on the counter and stared at him. "The golf club, where you go twice a week with your buddies to plot your latest takeover? The place you take every other female? You have to be joking."

Ron reached over and stroked the back of her hand, which got exactly the reaction he had expected. Linda snatched her hand away and took a step back. "Ron, no. I'm busy. Go away."

"I want to talk about the divorce settlement."

She looked at him suspiciously. "I'm not budging. For heaven's sake, Ron, we both know that you're richer than Croesus. You've got way more hidden away than I could ever hope to get at." A bitter smile creased her face. "I've overheard a couple of drunken conversations, and Yvonne has spilled a bit more. But you know what? You can keep it—*most* of it. I'm sure you've broken plenty of laws to get it. But I—" She broke off as a woman emerged from the cubicle and walked towards them.

Chris Baxter's face changed just a little as she spotted him. Stan Lambert had occasionally used her services to photograph real estate, making properties look bigger, brighter, and better than in real life. Ron had employed her too, once or twice.

"Hello, Ron," she said, her voice neutral.

"Chris!" He beamed at her. "Now, this is a happy coincidence. The boys and I were talking about you only yesterday. Were your ears burning?"

"Can't say they were." Dismissing him, she reached into her handbag for her wallet and turned to Linda. "Linda, put in that necklace that I tried on, will you? It'll go with quite a few things in my wardrobe."

Not fazed by her attitude, Ron leaned back against the counter and folded his arms. "Yep, we've got a few brochures to revamp and a couple of new ones. Stan was going to give you a call."

Chris didn't look at him. "I'm not doing any real estate work at the moment. I'm focusing on more creative stuff and my classes."

"Oh? That's a shame; we like to keep it local when we can. Never mind, we'll use Kat Morris in Maclean."

"Good choice. She's used to working with people like you." Chris's voice was polite, but he got the message. So did Linda, judging by the slight twitch at the corners of her lips.

Fine, he thought. Let them play their silly little games, enjoy a moment of petty triumph. He'd walk away from this divorce knowing that Linda was barely getting one-tenth of his net worth.

"Kat is focusing on real estate now," he said pleasantly. "She's one of the best out there."

They ignored him, and the door opened again. He stifled a sigh of frustration while a girl put several packages on the counter and then disappeared into the backroom, muttering something about unpacking the new stock.

*Aha.* Linda's latest casual assistant. Perfect timing.

He waited until Chris picked up her purchases and left, with a meaningful look back at Linda. No doubt one of those secret women's messages like *I'll go so you can get rid of him.*

The moment the door closed behind her, Linda put her hands on her hips, cast a look at the backroom, and said, still keeping her voice low, "Ron, you have to go. I'm running a business, we no longer married, and I don't want to see you."

"That may be the case," he said easily, turning on

the smile that had won her over two years before, "but I need to see *you*. If you want everything you're asking for in the divorce settlement, then I advise you to give me fifteen minutes of your precious time."

"I'm working."

"Take a lunch break. Your girl can watch the store."

Linda ran her fingers through her hair, her face a study in frustration. "Why can't we do this on the phone?"

*Because I can wear you down more easily in person*, he thought, and said, "Because I'm here now, and I want to get this over and done with. Just like you. Come on, Linda." He projected sincerity with a touch of helplessness, a ploy that had worked well with some clients in the past. "For old times sake. Let's see if we can settle this like adults."

"I can't take too long."

He shrugged. "Fine. We'll just grab a crepe and a coffee next door."

Linda frowned. "I don't want to talk in public."

"I don't plan to shout it from the rooftops. We can sit outside, in the corner with the pot plants."

Her lips tightened. "All right. Fifteen minutes."

------------------------------

18

# Linda

------------------------------

GEORGIE WAS about to phone Scott and suggest he come by for lunch when she saw Linda from next door sit down at an outside table. She was with a smiling man with a shiny bald head, who picked up a menu, glanced at it, said a few words, and then came inside.

He nodded at her, the laughter lines at the corners of his eyes creasing, and said: "Two crêpes, please—one chicken and avocado, one vegetarian. And two lattes." He gestured toward the window. "We're outside."

Georgie rang up the sale and handed him a number. "It won't take long."

Watching him go out, she saw an unsmiling Linda glance up. She said a few words and then sat back in her chair, her posture stiff.

The cafe was half full, and a good number of those present were locals. Georgie didn't miss the rolled eyes and inclined head from one of the women and the interest of two others sitting at an inside table near the window.

You didn't have to be Einstein to know that the two

out there had a history, and after being in close company with Scott's sisters for a week, she was willing to bet that the mystery man was probably Linda's ex-husband.

And despite the open face and smiling eyes, she knew at a gut level that he was untrustworthy.

She took the order to Viv in the kitchen. "Viv? Can you take a peek at the man with Linda and tell me who it is?"

"Sure." Viv picked up two plates with steaming hot crêpes on them and took them out to the dining area. Her glance at the window was casual, but the two outside were engrossed in their conversation anyway. The man was relaxed, confident, gesturing as he spoke. Linda's brows were drawn together in an unreceptive frown.

Viv came over to Georgie where she was busy behind the counter. "Name's Ron Foley. Linda's ex-husband, all-round creep. Ladies man, even when he was married." She wrinkled her nose. "*Especially* when he was married. Big wheel in the town, owner of the bottle-o, stocks vintage spirits. He made a play for Lissa at one stage, but she slapped him down." She disappeared back into the kitchen.

Well, that accounted for the stir of interest in the cafe. Georgie made their lattes and took them outside, setting them down with a smile.

"Hi, Linda." She nodded at the man with her, not revealing that she knew who he was. 'The crêpes will be ready shortly."

Linda flashed a brief smile, but as Georgie went back inside, she heard her say, "Let's drop the small talk, Ron. We're way past that. Just say what you have to say."

Another customer came in, and then another, and Georgie had to focus on coffee again.

But her antenna was up, and the increased awareness zinging in her veins told her that Ron Foley was not someone she should ignore.

---

Looking at Linda, Ron found himself wondering why he had ever wanted to marry her. He considered that for a moment while she stared at her coffee, not speaking. When he'd first met her, he had been attracted by Linda's soft, cultured voice and her classic blonde good looks. On the rebound from a charming but feckless husband, she had easily been won over by Ron's friendly, forthright approach and canny business sense.

Linda had contributed the proceeds of her apartment in Sydney to the marriage, along with a determination to run her own business in her way. Hence the little fashion boutique he had encouraged her to open—in a building owned by his good friend Stan Lambert, which Stan now wanted empty.

Which *all* of their little group wanted empty, because it was part of a mega, *mega* deal with a developer.

Women. Romance 'em, get what you want, but don't marry 'em, he thought. That would be his new rule to live by. He planned to keep all his money.

Jim Beggs had been smart, keeping Maureen in the dark all these years.

The American girl came back out with the crêpes, and he waited for her to go before he said to Linda, "I know you're mad at me. And I'll be the first to admit I haven't been a saint."

Linda let out a sarcastic crack of laughter.

"Yeah, all right, fair enough." He maintained eye contact and a pleasant expression. "But let's try to remain civil and get this settled. We both want to move on, right?"

"Why, Ron." She fluttered her eyelashes at him and then glared. "That's the first conciliatory statement I've heard from you in months."

He ignored that. "You want the house. OK. You can have the house. You want the BMW; you want the entire investment in the business. I'm on board with that. Those things alone come to more than your initial investment in our marriage in the first place, agreed?"

Linda cut into the crêpe and ate a mouthful, looking at him and saying nothing.

"Come on, work with me here, Lins."

"It's *Linda.*"

"Fine. Linda." Ron kept forking his crêpe into his mouth as though he didn't have a concern in the world but observed her carefully. "I'll agree to all of that, no contest, *plus…*" he paused to give what he was about to say great impact. "…the entire balance of our joint account as it stood the day before I moved out."

He swallowed a mouthful of chicken and avocado and smiled at her placidly.

Linda put down her knife and fork. She did a creditable job of trying to hide the shock in her eyes, but he saw it anyway. "Are you saying what I think you're saying? You're giving it *back*?"

"Not right away," he said quickly. There was no way he could spare that amount right now. "But it'll be part of the settlement. Almost two hundred grand and change, as I recall." He conjured up an expression of regret. "I concede that what I did wasn't entirely fair."

That earned him another eye roll from his ex. "What's the catch?"

"There's no *catch*. No downside for you in this at all. I'm wearing my business hat, but I make no apologies for that." Ron put on his *I-am-completely-honest-and-transparent* face. "Stan's got some big deals in the wings. To raise capital, he needs to sell off some of his properties."

The expression in Linda's eyes changed, and he saw her put two and two together. She glanced through the cafe window, where they could see the American girl serving someone who was pointing at the cake display, and then she looked at her shop next door. "Including this building. That's what's going on, isn't it?"

"It's not the only one. He's taking a big risk, but—" He shrugged, inviting her to join in an understanding of the situation. "You know Stan. Nothing ventured, nothing gained. One of these days, he's going to fall flat on his face, but in the meantime, it's to my advantage to help make it happen."

Linda picked up her knife and fork and placed them neatly together on her plate, even though she'd eaten only a few bites.

Ron didn't like the look of that.

"Let me guess," she said. "This generous offer of yours. It's a bribe to encourage me to move out, isn't it?"

"Give me a break. You know that Stan and I have been partners for a long time. If I can do this small thing to help him, then why not? He tells me he's prepared to cut you a deal on the rental of the property over near the mall."

"And all of this is purely to do a favor for your...."

Linda made air quotes with her fingers *"good friend Stan"*? There's nothing in it for you?" She looked at him scornfully. "Pull the other leg, Ron. You're buying into this deal of his, aren't you?"

Ron heaved a frustrated sigh and shook his head. Did she honestly expect him to admit to it? "You're an intelligent woman, Linda, but you never did get how all of this works. I do Stan a favor now to get something he wants, and somewhere down the track—even if it's years away—he'll help me out when I need it."

"So you'll agree to everything that I've asked for, no argument, and throw in the best part of two hundred grand on top of it? Just to do Stan a favor?"

He shrugged. "All right, so I'm letting my heart rule my head." He didn't think Linda was smart enough to know that she could get most of that two hundred grand anyway if she had the right lawyer. Or a great deal more than that, if anyone really started digging.

He was trying to avoid that at all costs. Offering her two hundred grand and caving in on the rest of the divorce settlement should keep her sweet.

It'd keep Stan Lambert sweet, too, because he was too much of a Scrooge to pay out his tenants' lease, especially when things were so tight.

Looking at her, he could see that Linda didn't seem to be entirely convinced. All right, time to get tough.

"I think it's worth letting you have the two hundred grand if it means we can part on amicable terms *and* both get something out of it." He leaned forward in his seat, searching her eyes. "It's going to save you a lot of stress, Linda. But if you play hardball, you'll be in a world of hurt." As he said it, he let a hint of threat into his gaze.

She might as well be reminded of who she was dealing with.

Linda sat silently for a moment, staring at him, her light blue eyes cool. Then her gaze moved to the logo of the coffee cup on the window behind them and through the glass to the people sitting inside. "And what about Viv and Lissa? What happens to them?"

"What happens to them is not your concern. Worry about yourself. If it relieves your conscience, Stan has offered them the same rental deal in the new place."

"It won't work for them any better than it will work for me, moving away from the township."

Ron couldn't have cared less what happened to *Coffee, Cakes, and Crêpes*. He didn't care what happened to Linda's little dress shop either.

But he could pretend to. He could feed her any misinformation he felt like.

"All right. I'll tell you something, but this must go no further." He glanced around and then lowered his voice. "Stan has some big plans for the area over there near the mall. If you breathe a word, it could wreck every-thing, so this has to stay between us. But if you're smart and move now, you'll be sitting pretty. And so will those Mowbray girls." He jerked his head in the direction of the patrons inside the cafe. "They'll be getting more customers than they can deal with."

"What kind of plans?"

"I can't tell you that." Ron finished off the last of his crêpe. "Told you too much already. You can't say a word to *anyone*."

Linda picked up her handbag and pushed her chair back.

Ron cocked his head and looked at her inquiringly. "Well? Are we having a conversation here?"

She stood up and looked down at him. "We're having a conversation, but something smells bad to me. The girls here have been having a lot of bad luck recently, Ron. You wouldn't know anything about that, would you?"

Ron stood up, so he was looking straight at her, his face unsmiling. "Of course not. And I wouldn't be spreading rumors like that around either, if I were you. Think carefully about my offer, Linda, because it's not going to be open for long. I'll call you tonight."

With that, he turned and walked off.

------

19

# Coffee Class

------

AT TWO FIFTY-FIVE on Sunday afternoon, Maureen Beggs picked up her handbag and car keys and headed for the door. She didn't say a single word to Jim, who was clashing pots and pans in the kitchen.

Her husband was barely speaking to her. Once, that would have made her feel sick and anxious. Now, she had to choke down an insane desire to laugh.

She didn't *care* that Jim Beggs was playing no-talkies. Nor did she care that he'd disappeared for an hour right before the lunch-time rush, when their current back-packer, Anton, breezed in to relieve him.

Anton was young, handsome, liked to talk to the customers, and could make great coffee. Win-win, as far as she was concerned.

After Jim stalked out of the door, Maureen had caught a glimpse of him climbing into a sleek silver Audi that purred off immediately. She knew who owned that car: Ron Foley, one of Jim's oldest mates, who rarely bothered to give her the time of day. Jim was off to play golf again, but this time it seemed he was leaving early.

To punish her, no doubt.

She'd already asked Anton to work from three o'clock anyway, so she could join the barista class across the road, but as it turned out, there was no need. Jim came back at two-thirty, told Anton to go, and turned his back on Maureen.

*No golf?* She was stunned.

Was Jim there just to see what she was doing? Had Anton told him about being asked to work at three o'clock?

*Fine.* She didn't care. She wasn't going to hide what she did anymore.

She could feel his eyes boring into her back as she left, and was quite sure that he would have watched her walk across the road and into *Coffee, Cakes & Crepes,* which always closed early on Sundays so Lissa could run her barista class.

Lissa looked up and sent her a genuinely welcoming smile. "Maureen! You made it. Excellent. By the time we've finished with you, you'll be good enough to enter competitions." She gestured to the half-dozen women sitting in a group, chatting. Irene and Janet were sitting on the sofa with a woman Maureen didn't know, and two others were probably people from the caravan park.

The other one was Linda Malloy from the shop next door, which surprised her. Although Jim and Linda's ex-husband were as thick as thieves, she and Linda didn't have much in common. Linda wasn't exactly snobbish, but she made Maureen feel plain and uninteresting.

Which, if she were to be honest, she *was.*

With that depressing thought in mind, Maureen hesitantly went over to join them.

"Maureen Beggs! Over here again?" Irene said bluntly. "Having more time off?"

Before she had time to answer, someone took her elbow from behind, and a laughing American voice said, "We twisted her arm, Irene. Maureen's doing so well, Lissa persuaded her to come so she could show her some extra touches."

Unaccountably touched by the support from Georgie, Maureen put her chin in the air and looked Irene in the eye. "Jim likes to give his regulars percolated coffee, but he has to learn the world's moved on. Wouldn't you agree?"

"Still and all, I never thought I'd see the day. And doesn't Jim play golf on Sundays?" Irene looked as though she was going to push it further, but Lissa's voice cut in.

"I think we're all here, so if you'd all like to come out to the kitchen? I'll demonstrate, show you some of the new syrups, and it seems you all want to know how to make pretty pictures on the top...."

There was a ripple of laughter and a chorus of yeses, and everyone got up to troop out to the kitchen.

Lissa had four coffee machines set up, all different brands, so that they could experiment on all of them. They rotated, two people per machine, with a different partner each time so they could get to know each other.

They practiced grinding the beans, tamping the coffee, stretching the milk, testing the temperature, and —the most popular part—creating nifty designs on the crema when they poured in the milk.

At that point, Maureen found herself teamed with Irene Wilson.

Usually, she avoided Irene. If she were honest, she

was more than a little scared of that sharp tongue. Today, though, she felt braver. Just enough to be able to smile and say, "This is the bit I want to know how to do. Our latest backpacker is fantastic at it."

"Yes, he made a cup of coffee for me yesterday." Irene efficiently tamped the coffee, clicked in the portafilter, and pressed a button. When the coffee had finished streaming into the cup, she poured milk into the stainless steel jug and swiveled the milk wand towards herself. "So, Jim has admitted defeat on the coffee issue?"

"He had to," Maureen said. "If the customers can't get it, they go somewhere else."

"Wise of him." Irene steamed the milk, watching carefully until it stretched to fill the jug. "You still have the best fish and chips in town, but why not get the coffee crowd as well?"

Maureen blinked. "You really think so? About the fish and chips?"

"Wouldn't say so if it wasn't true." Irene put her tongue between her teeth. "Okay, here we go. *Please* let it work this time!" She poured the milk into the cup, then jiggled it as Lissa had shown them, only to end up with a shapeless squiggle on the top. "Oh, *darn* it! This isn't as easy as it looks!" She looked up in disgust.

Amused, Maureen grinned. "I don't think I'll do any better, but here goes."

It was Irene's turn to watch, and she used the time to keep probing. "What does Jim think about you coming over here?"

"Not happy," Maureen admitted, growing in concentration. "Sssh, Irene, if I talk, I get it wrong." She inserted the milk wand into the jug and touched the button.

Within seconds, she was staring in disappointment at the results.

Bubbles. *Bubbles.*

"Oh, man." She put the jug down and ran a hand through her hair. "No wonder everyone keeps leaving to walk over here for coffee. What with Jim's percolated stuff that's strong enough to start a car, and my *bubbles…* I'll never get it."

"Oh yes, you will," came Lissa's voice in her ear. "I've seen you do it. It's just practice. Watch." She smiled at Irene. "I'll make another one from scratch, and *you*"— with a finger pointing at Maureen—"will learn to stretch the milk, while *you*"—Irene's turn—"will be able to create a perfect design. And neither of you two ladies is leaving until you've come up with the goods."

Maureen and Irene looked at each other, and everyone listening had a good laugh, and then they exchanged a grin themselves. Unaccountably Maureen felt a surge of something inside her that was so foreign that she scarcely recognized it.

Happiness.

A simple thing like going to a barista class made her *happy.*

Twenty minutes later, when she finally produced a decent cappuccino with a respectable design on the top, she felt even happier.

Enough to say to Irene, "Come in tomorrow, and I'll practice on you." Belatedly, she remembered that Irene was usually joined at the hip with Janet. "And Janet, too, of course."

"It'll have to be after lunch," Irene said. "I've got my quilting group in the morning."

"I know," Maureen said. "I'll be there too. So afternoon is fine."

"You'll be there? I didn't know you could quilt." Irene stared at her, and when she glanced around, Maureen found that Linda Malloy was also looking surprised.

No wonder. For years—or was it centuries?—all she had done was work in the cafe, cook fish and chips, and make sandwiches.

"I can't," she said. "I'm coming to learn."

Irene being Irene, she couldn't resist asking. "And what does your Jim think of that?"

"He doesn't know," Maureen said. She straightened her spine and cast Irene a quelling look. "He won't like it, because let's face it, Jim doesn't like *anything*, but I don't care. I need something more than fish and chips in my life." She picked up her cup and saucer to take them to the sink and couldn't resist adding, "Even if they are the best in Yamba."

"Well." Irene put her hands on her hips in an exaggerated expression of astonishment. "The worm has turned. Good on you, Maureen Beggs."

On the way to the sink, Maureen caught Linda Malloy's eye. She had a slight smile on her lips, and she nodded at Maureen and then gave her a thumbs up.

Astonished, Maureen added her cup to the stack waiting to be rinsed and put in the dishwasher.

Linda Malloy giving her a seal of approval?

What was that about?

---

20

## Jim Fumes

---

When Maureen walked out of the cafe just before three, Jim at first thought that she was doing it just to get back at him for leaving her with the lunchtime crowd.

The woman had gone mad. Ever since her mother had died, she had changed. So much for him sending money to the old bag to help her out. Did Maureen show the proper level of appreciation for that?

No. A big, fat **NO**.

Admittedly, he'd get all his money back, and then some, once probate went through, but that was beside the point. He didn't *have* to pay the medical bills and send money to make her life a bit more comfortable; he'd done it out of the goodness of his heart.

And look at what he got in return.

Push, push, push all the time, telling him they had to move with the times; serve all this rubbish that Maureen said the tourists wanted.

*He* knew what they wanted. Good old-fashioned, well-cooked fish and chips. How many times had people told him that his fish and chips were the best for miles around?

But no, Maureen had to spend money on a coffee machine without even asking him before she dipped into their joint account. She'd started ordering cakes from the bakery, not even decent stuff like custard slices and cream buns, but silly little things called friands and oversized muffins filled with fruit or banana and white chocolate.

And cupcakes.

He directed a furious glance across the road, where Maureen had gone.

To *Coffee, Cakes & Crepes,* a fussy name to go with a frippery little business.

To *those girls.*

He knew they closed the cafe early on Sundays to run those coffee-making classes, and he'd seen Irene Wilson and Janet Cox going in, along with a couple of touristy-looking types *and* Linda Malloy.

Linda Malloy.

Grumpily, Jim automatically filled a couple of orders while he mulled over what Linda Malloy and his Maureen were doing over there.

He didn't like it. Didn't like it one bit.

He didn't think Ron was quite as careful about keeping secrets as he was, and he wouldn't be surprised if Linda knew about some of their investments in common.

What if Maureen found out?

That morning, Ron had filled him in on the latest: his generous offer aimed at getting Linda out of the building, and her annoying refusal to commit when he'd phoned her last night.

Ron was reasonably sure that she'd take it—who would say 'no' to an extra two hundred grand?—but he was going to keep the pressure on to make sure.

Women, they agreed, were more trouble than they were worth. Ron had spent some time pointing out the advantages of not being tied down to one of them.

Jim slapped the customers' orders down in front of them, took their money, and found his eyes going again to the window of *Coffee, Cakes & Crepes*, where he could see women milling around inside before they all sat at tables and talked their heads off.

Just *wait* until Maureen came back. He wasn't going to put up with this. She could either pull her weight, or she could move out.

He allowed himself to toy with that idea. As Ron had pointed out, he could get a housekeeper, play golf whenever he wanted, get backpackers in to do Maureen's job. Or maybe not backpackers, perhaps someone from the town on a permanent basis. He'd have to pay them, but he wouldn't have to put up with Maureen's disapproval.

He'd have a yarn to Ron about that. After all, Ron had managed to hide a lot from Linda, just as he had from Maureen.

---

At four-thirty, Maureen returned, carrying shiny foil bags of coffee beans and juggling a large cardboard box with a picture of a coffee machine on it. Jim, with three customers waiting and the usual Sunday afternoon take-away crowd due in, had been on the verge of charging across the road to drag her back rather than giving Anton a call.

Maureen heaved the box on the counter, cheerfully greeting the customers. Her eyes met Jim's, and there wasn't a hint of apology there.

Instead, he saw defiance.

Maureen lifted the flap on the counter, let herself through, and took the box out into the kitchen before tying on her apron. Silently, she got to work.

Jim couldn't hold it back any longer. "And what's that you've got *now*?"

Maureen didn't look at him. "A coffee machine."

"We've *got* a coffee machine. You insisted on spending money on the blasted thing. What do we need another one for?"

"The first one was for the cafe. This one's for home, so I can practice. And because I *enjoy* a cup of decent coffee."

"Instant's good enough for most people," he ground out.

"Well, actually, it's not, Jim. Not these days. Anyway, I used my own money, so it's not your call." With that, she went out and started taking orders.

Jim slapped fish into batter viciously. Divorce was starting to sound like a very tempting option.

Right after her mother's money came through. Then he would take back what was rightfully his before booting her out.

And that wasn't *all* he was going to do.

Jim fumed, and prepared fish and chips, and plotted.

While she automatically exchanged banter with customers and smiled at them while she wrote down their orders, Maureen's mind was racing. She thought of the fun she'd had that afternoon, and how she'd held her own with Irene Wilson, and how she'd defied Jim to do what she wanted—and *buy* what she wanted—and how good it felt.

Why was she even thinking of waiting two months to retire? And why was she hesitating to take control of her own life? She could set things in motion now and spend her birthday celebrating her freedom.

Tomorrow, after she went to the quilting group, she would go and see Linda Malloy.

Linda was going through a divorce. She'd be able to pass on some advice about what Jim could and couldn't lay claim to.

Maybe she could have either the investment duplex or the house, *all for herself.*

She didn't care about the old cafe, because she had her mother's money.

Life was strange, no doubt about that. Who would have thought that she and Linda, so poles apart in personality and life choices, would both be divorcing two conniving old schoolmates?

# 21

# A-Quilting We Will Go

ELEVEN PEOPLE TURNED up to Adele's quilting group, held in the converted garage at the back of her house. The morning was filled with banter and gossip, and Georgie found that everyone had an opinion on what she should use as a design for the Yamba square on her "Around Australia" quilt.

It was fun, but by the time everyone was packing up, she still had no clue why the quilting group should be important. She had covertly studied all the women present, but even after a few hours, she had no idea why she was there. Nobody seemed to be making anything with flowers on it, either.

Could she have been completely wrong? Maybe it wasn't this group. Perhaps it wasn't *any* group, and the vision of women passing around the quilted square had meant something else entirely.

Then it was time for them all to pack up and go to lunch at a waterside restaurant—and it was there that Georgie finally understood.

Watching rain spattering against the restaurant windows, Georgie thought nervously of Louise's predictions after reading the cards. She had foreseen trouble with water—which, she said, could be related to bad weather.

Across the river, heavy dark storm clouds were moving in. She wasn't sure whether Scott had remembered to check the roof of the house and the cafe in case of leaks; she must remember to mention that to him when she got back.

At lunch, she made sure she sat next to Maureen. They knew each other well enough now for Georgie to be able to steer the conversation in the direction she wanted it to go.

"Maureen, you said something at the barista class yesterday about retiring soon?" She smiled at her. "Does that mean you have a birthday coming up, or are you just sick of work?" *Or sick of Jim,* she added silently.

"Two months to go," Maureen said, looking both excited and nervous. She glanced at Irene, two seats away, who was trying to pretend she wasn't listening in. "That's when my birthday is. I had just kind of settled on retiring at 65, but..." she lowered her voice. "Just yesterday, I was thinking, why wait? What difference does it make?"

Georgie was pretty certain it would make a difference to her husband, but she refrained from saying so. "You're sixty-five in a couple of months? I hope you've let them know at *Coffee, Cakes, and Crepes.* You get a free coffee and a cupcake on your birthday from now on, did you know?"

Irene turned in their direction. "Lissa made us all write down our birthdays yesterday. I'll be getting my freebies before you, Maureen. Mine's in…" she counted on her fingers. "Ten days."

"Is it?" Georgie turned to her with an encouraging smile. "What star sign does that make you, Irene?"

"Aquarius. Which is supposed to make me impulsive and charming." Irene laughed. "Well, I'm certainly impulsive, but the jury's out on the charm."

Perfect opening, thought Georgie. "What about you, Maureen? What does your star sign say?"

"Aries," she said. "But I'm nothing like I'm supposed to be…impulsive and energetic and domineering. I hate conflict. I just like a quiet life."

Aha. Georgie almost felt like punching the air. Louise had definitely said *Aries*–someone amenable; she'd said, someone who liked to please others.

Bingo. What else had she said? There was someone connected with Maureen, who was older, someone more intense and determined. And impatient?

Georgie thought about how to approach it and then grinned to herself. *Intense, determined, impatient?* Right.

She began to talk about her Great Grandma Rosa.

Maureen was fascinated, listening to her story. "I can't believe it. You and your great-grandma–you both read *crystal balls*? Does that mean you can tell the future?"

"Sometimes," Georgie admitted. "I could wish it was more accurate, but that's the way it goes."

"But you really can see things?" The expression in Maureen's eyes showed both wonder and curiosity. "Would you be able to see what's in store for me?"

"Quite possibly." Conscious that Irene was now

openly listening, Georgie quickly added, "I usually approach it as a fun thing, and if I find out anything that might help, it's a bonus."

"I'd like to do that. If that's okay."

"Of course you can." Inwardly, Georgie was elated. It was always much easier if someone was keen, rather than having to be talked into reading. "When would you like to do it?"

Maureen chewed on her lip, thinking. "We close the cafe at eight. I could come then. Is tonight too soon?"

"Tonight would be fine. In fact…" She thought of Scott. He knew how to do an astrological spread, just like his mother. "Why don't we combine it with a card reading as well? My partner, Scott, does those. He learned from his mom—she's an astrologer."

Maureen's eyes glowed. "A crystal ball reading *and* a card reading? How exciting! I always visited the tarot reader at the markets, but I never told Jim about it. He doesn't believe in that stuff."

Georgie reflected that Jim Beggs probably didn't believe in anything that would afford his wife pleasure. How Maureen had managed to stay with him for decades, she had no idea.

"We'll make it a date, then," she said. "Come down as soon as the shop closes. We're staying in the caravan park, but I'll walk up to the entrance and wait for you at around eight, show you where to go."

*Now,* she thought. Back to her great-grandmother's personality, so she could find out what she wanted to know. "Rosa's an amazing woman, but I was scared of her for years. She is quite abrupt, very determined—and always speaks her mind." She gave a wry laugh. "I'm sure you know the type."

"Oh, I do." Maureen nodded vigorously. "You could be talking about my mother–God rest her soul." An expression of sadness crossed her face, and she added softly, "She passed away a couple of months ago."

"I'm sorry to hear that." Georgie squeezed Maureen's hand, wondering if her mother had been the last support she had against Jim. "You must miss her."

"She didn't live here. She had a house in Maclean, but she was determined not to be pushed into a retirement home. She loved her garden, and she couldn't bear the thought of not having one. She had vases of flowers everywhere. Well, she got her wish." Maureen toyed with the lunch and roll on her plate, remembering. "She stayed in her own home until she died, although the last few months were difficult. I drove there to see her when I could, and Jim sent money to help her out."

"I'm sure your mother must've appreciated that. Both the visits and the financial assistance."

"She liked seeing me, but...." Maureen shrugged, and her mouth twisted in a slightly bitter line. "She blamed Jim for not letting me see her more often, although he was all right with me staying with her for the last couple of weeks of her life." Her eyes met Georgie's. "Jim is not an easy man to like, and my mother couldn't abide him. And, like your great-grandma, she wasn't backward in speaking her mind. Thought I should have left him years ago."

"Well, obviously, you didn't agree," Georgie said gently. "And everyone has to make up their own mind."

"He wasn't always quite as bad as he is now," Maureen said. "He worked hard, and I was happy to work hard alongside him to secure our retirement. Fish and chips in a country cafe...it's not a recipe for riches."

She stared at the raindrops trickling down the window. "But now... I'm beginning to think my mother was right."

Although she and Maureen were sitting at the end of the table, Georgie had the feeling that Irene, a few seats away, was straining to catch the conversation.

She cast about for a way to find out the last piece of information she needed. "It sounds as though you and your mother had very different personalities," she said. "Just out of interest, what star sign was she?"

"I don't know," Maureen admitted. "Her birthday is on the nineteenth of May."

"The nineteenth," Georgie repeated. "I'll ask Scott. He'll know."

Irene's head swung towards them. "Did I hear you talking about star signs? The nineteenth of May? My sister's birthday is on the fourteenth of May. That's Taurus."

*Taurus*. Georgie felt a surge of triumph. Maureen was Aries, and her mother was Taurus. She had the right two women.

Then she had a sudden image of the basket of flowers on the quilting square in the crystal ball. Flowers, of course—Maureen said her mother had loved them. It was all coming together. Now she just had to figure out what Maureen's mother had to do with all this.

"Taurus? Thanks, Irene," Georgie said, hiding a grin. She glanced at Maureen and found that she, too, had an amused glint in her eye.

Well, that was Irene. You didn't earn the title of town gossip unless you listened in at every opportunity.

"You said you're an Aquarian, didn't you, Irene?"

she asked. Time to direct the conversation away from Maureen. "Have you ever had your astrological chart done?"

"I have," Irene said, "and now I'm going to insist that you do a reading with your crystal ball, too, just like you are for Maureen. See if you come up with the same things...." Within that, Irene took the floor, and they were hearing all about her path through life and what the tarot card reader at the markets had told her.

All in all, Georgie thought, a successful day. Maureen was coming out of her shell, and Georgie had achieved quite a lot. First, she'd learned that Maureen and her mother fit the birthday profiles. Second, Maureen had agreed to a reading tonight, and Georgie was certain that would yield more information about her mother.

Third... clearly, Jim Beggs had been keeping secrets from his wife. According to Scott's brother, Jim had several investments with Stan Lambert–he of the "owns half of the Yamba" fame.

Yet Maureen seemed convinced that they wouldn't have a lot of money for their retirement.

Someone didn't understand what was going on, and she was willing to bet it wasn't Jim.

# 22

# Jim Blows His Top

AFTER TAKING off to suit herself the day before to attend that stupid coffee class, Maureen had disappeared *again*. One minute she was at the front counter taking orders, and the next, she was gone.

Jim turned around to find that instead of his prune-faced wife coming through the kitchen doorway with the orders, it was Anton.

Jim stared at him, his blood immediately heating up. "What are *you* doing here?"

Already used to Jim's ways and not the slightest bit intimidated, Anton shrugged. "Your wife asked me to work today, from eight-thirty through till one-thirty." He angled his wristwatch at Jim and pointed. "It's right on eight-thirty."

Jim pushed past him and went to the door, opening it just in time to see Maureen's little white Holden Barina disappearing up the street.

Where the hell was she off to now? This was getting ridiculous. *Ridiculous.*

He stomped back inside and, ignoring the two old

men drinking tea in a corner booth and two women at the counter, demanded, "Did she say where she's going?"

"No. Just asked me to come in between eight-thirty and one-thirty; that's all I know." Unconcerned, Anton got the milk out of the fridge and went to the coffee machine to fix the women's orders.

Anton might not have known where Maureen was, but others in the town did, it seemed. By eleven o'clock, he had found out that she had gone off to spend the morning with some craft group. At twelve-thirty, a woman ordering fried calamari rings announced that she'd seen Maureen having lunch at the restaurant by the river, sitting next to that American woman who had been working in the cafe across the road.

Jim gritted his teeth and said nothing, but he *thought* plenty.

When there was a lull just before one-thirty, he motioned Anton into the kitchen, folded his arms, and stared at him.

"You said you knew the backpacker I had working in here before, name of Nick."

Anton nodded, his dark eyes keen.

"He told you to come here and ask here for work. That right?"

"Said if I knew how to cook fried food, make coffee, I should be fine."

Jim's eyebrows lowered. This was where he had to be careful. "Did he tell you about any other tasks I asked him to do?"

A slow smile grew on Anton's face. "He might have."

"None of this *might have* business," snapped Jim. "Did he or didn't he?"

Anton waited for a beat for he spoke, staring at Jim, spinning it out. "He said that you could be very generous to staff who could help out in other ways." He leaned against the door jamb and looked pointedly at the cafe across the road. "You like to make sure there are no cockroaches on *your* premises, for example."

Jim grunted. "And what was your response to that?"

"I thought this sounded like the kind of place I'd like to work," Anton said. "I need money for travel. I don't care how I get it."

Jim nodded. His instincts had been right. "I'll pay you fifty bucks to do a job right now."

"If it's the same kind of job that Nick did," Anton said coolly, "you paid him a hundred."

Jim bit back a retort and contented himself with a glare instead. It would be worth a hundred bucks if it worked. If not—well then, he would just have to think of something else.

"All right, but if you get caught, you keep your mouth shut."

"I won't get caught."

"Right. Get yourself over there now; order something to eat. And then —"

"Who's going to pay for the food?"

"I will," Jim growled. "But make sure it's something cheap."

Anton nodded. "Cockroaches again?"

"No," Jim said. "This time, I'm trying something different. Come with me."

Trev Chaffey had not had a good morning. He had started work at six-thirty, and a job that was supposed to take an hour and a half, tops, had spun out closer to four hours—one of those situations where one problem led to another lead to another. That had made him late for his second job of the day, so he'd missed his usual morning cappuccino from *Coffee, Cakes, and Crêpes.*

At the second job on a building site, he couldn't get started until the concreters had finished, and because they were running late too, he had to stand around waiting…but didn't dare leave the site in case someone else arrived to snag his place in the queue. *Then* the clouds had started building, and the rain started.

Just one of those days. Now it was well after one-thirty, he'd had to reschedule the third job of the day, and he had twenty minutes before he was due at number four, which looked like being rained out anyway.

He was frustrated and starving, and although fish and chips would have gone down well, he figured he would feel better after seeing Viv's slow, warm smile rather than Maureen Beggs' unhappy face. And Viv *did* do a pretty good job on the crêpes.

He went to *Coffee, Cakes & Crêpes*, and something went right for the first time that day. Although there were still a few people lingering over coffee, most of the lunchtime crowd had been taken care of, so Viv had time to come out and chat. She'd been doing that occasionally now, when he came in, and Trevor was beginning to think maybe she liked him for his own sake, not just because he'd helped them out a few times when things went wrong.

"Hi, Trev." Viv slid his cheese and bacon crêpe in

front of him, and a moment later, Lissa arrived with his cappuccino, plus one for her sister. She squeezed Viv's shoulder. "Take five, Viv. Everything is quiet."

The twin aromas of bacon and coffee tantalized Trev's nose, and he heaved a huge sigh as he picked up his knife and fork. "Man, do I need this."

As he tucked in, Viv smiled at him. "Been a rough day?"

"You don't know the half of it." Briefly, in between wolfing down the crêpe, he filled her in.

Half amused and a half rueful, she grinned sympathetically. "We all have days like that."

Right then, they heard a rumble of thunder, and the rain started coming down in earnest.

"And there goes job number four," said Trev, feeling resigned. "I might as well have stayed in bed this morning." He picked up his cup of coffee, feeling guilty for complaining when the girls had had such a rough time of it. "Anyway, tomorrow is another day. How are things going with you guys? Everything settled down now?"

Viv rolled her eyes. "I would say yes, but I don't like tempting fate."

Behind her, the door opened, and the backpacker who'd been doing a bit of part-time work across the road walked in. *Don't order a crêpe*, thought Trev. He didn't want Viv to have to jump up and return to the kitchen.

"You might have just had one of those bad runs," Trev suggested. "Happens to us all. I remember when I had all my tools stolen, right after two weeks of bad weather that held up most of the work around here. You get through it."

A moment later, Lissa came over to them. "Sorry,

Viv. He wants a vegetarian crêpe. I'd make it for you, but I've got two more lattes to do."

"That's okay. It won't take me long." She stood up and then paused, looking down at Trevor. "If you don't have to rush off, the kitchen closes at two. I can take a break for a while."

Her tone sounded casual, and her smile held no hint of anything else but friendship, but Trev's heart leaped in his chest.

"Might as well," he said in an offhand tone that matched hers. "All right, I'll hang about."

"Okay. Back soon." Viv disappeared, and Trev lifted the coffee cup to his mouth with a grin big enough to swallow the whole thing. His eye caught Lissa, and she winked and gave him a thumbs up.

Trev felt the blood rush to his face. Were his feelings for Viv that obvious? Did Viv herself know? What if she was just being kind?

Outside, the rain started coming down harder. Trev stared into his coffee and then took another gulp. He didn't want Viv to spend time with him as a kindness.

Opposite him, he heard the scrape of a chair being dragged back. He looked up to see Lissa sitting down. "Trev, I'm just gonna say this once, okay?"

Not knowing what to expect, he nodded and then, unable to look at her, glanced away. Over her shoulder, he could see the backpacker standing up and looking at some of the Yamba seascapes on the wall. He was jigging up and down, impatient for his lunch.

"Trev." Lissa's determined voice pulled his eyes back to hers. "Viv likes you a lot. I don't think she knows quite how *much* she likes you if you get my meaning."

Trev stared at her. He didn't know what to say.

"This business with Shane and Amber kind of wrecked her confidence, turned her off men. And Amber rubbing it in all the time makes her feel like an idiot."

"If you ask me," Trev said sharply, "it's Shane Carter who's the idiot. He's got a woman like Viv right in front of his eyes, and he lets her go for the sake of a twit like Amber Kaye? You don't know the number of times I felt like going down to the bakery to punch his lights out."

He averted his gaze from Lissa's again, afraid he'd given away too much.

The backpacker had moved on to a framed poster outlining the history of the area, but what caught Trev's attention was the way he took a quick look around, his gaze resting on the couple nearest to him, before glancing down at his feet. His head turned towards them, so Trev instinctively made sure his gaze was focused on Lissa. Out of the corner of his eye, he saw the guy return to his seat and sit down.

Something was off. Trev's mind went immediately to theft; while he knew perfectly well that most backpackers were fine, there was a certain number who funded their travels with a bit of petty theft.

But what could he steal from here while he was standing out in the open like that?

"Trev?" Lissa tapped him on the wrist. "Are you listening to me? Or am I totally off base here?"

"No. I mean yes." Dragging his mind back to what was important, he gathered together all his courage and set in a rush, "Are you saying that I might have a chance with Viv?"

Lissa shook her head in mock sadness. "Honestly,

men are so slow at times. Yes, Trev. I'm saying you have a chance with Viv. Ask her out, why don't you? But don't tell her I told you to. *Sssh*. Here she comes."

Lissa stood up and pointed at him as Viv walked past to take the aromatic crêpe over to the backpacker. "Stay there, Trev. It's raining outside, and you can't do any work, so settle yourself in and chat to Viv."

She sailed past her sister with a cheerful, "Go sit down; I'll bring coffee. If anyone else asks for crepes, the kitchen's now closed." Looking back over her shoulder, she called, "Another one for you too, Trev?"

He nodded, but his eyes went back to the backpacker.

Viv sank into the seat vacated by Lissa. "I'd love to sit down for a while. We've been on the run all day, and if you look outside, you'll see the tennis club ladies are about to take refuge from the rain in here too." She smiled at him ruefully. "I might have to jump up and help Lissa. Will you stay anyway?"

"Sure," he said. "Just give me a newspaper to read, and I'm cool."

His day had just improved a hundredfold.

His eyes went again to the backpacker. Something just didn't feel right—especially when the kid shoveled down the crepe as though he had twenty seconds to eat it, tossed down his coffee, and bounded out of the door, elbowing his way past the ladies from the tennis club.

He went straight back across the road and into Jim Beggs' cafe.

Why hadn't he eaten his lunch over there?

Trev frowned. On impulse, he stood up. "Just a second, Viv. There's something I want to check out."

------------------------------

23

Team Meeting

------------------------------

FIVE OF THEM gathered in the RV: Georgie, Scott, Lissa, Viv, and Trevor Chaffey. All five felt charged: things were coming to a head. Trev kept casting little looks at each of them as if he wasn't quite sure what he was doing there.

Georgie felt nerves getting the better of her. She didn't understand enough about what was going on, and she still didn't know who, precisely, was responsible for everything that had happened to Scott's sisters, although she had her suspicions.

They waited silently while Scott listened to his brother and scribbled on a pad of paper next to his elbow. "Uh-huh," he muttered. "*How* many investment properties? You're kidding. Okay. Birthdays?" He paused, nodding and listening, and looked at Georgie. "Sent an email. Right."

Georgie reached for her tablet and called up her email, and studied the document that Bluey had sent through. She passed it around so that the others could take a look too.

Finally, Scott hung up. His eyes were serious as he looked at Georgie. "Get this. From what Bluey has been able to find out, Jim Beggs is worth somewhere between one point five and two million. It could well be more than that, judging from the way he's been able to hide most of it."

Georgie's mouth opened in shock. "That much. Well, he's certainly hiding it from Maureen."

"There's more," Scott went on. "Ron Foley has played the same sort of games with his ex, Linda. She's much better off than Maureen Beggs, but she probably only knows a fraction of what Ron is worth. And both Jim and Ron are in deep with Stan Lambert and the local dentist, Stephen Patterson."

"It's pretty obvious that the four of them are tied to whatever has been happening with you two," Georgie said to Scott's sisters. "But how we can prove anything, I wouldn't have a clue. Nor do we know what else they might have planned. And who? Are they all in it, or just one? Or two?"

Trevor glanced at Viv and then the others. "At least we're not working in the dark now. Well, not totally."

"Largely thanks to you," Viv said, looking at him gratefully. "Those tennis women were about to sit down right where that horrible kid dropped the mouse pellets. There were so *many* of them... another health violation would have ruined us."

Trevor made a face. "I still wish you'd let me go over there to sort Beggs out."

"It wouldn't have achieved anything," Viv said, her tone dispirited. "Jim would never admit to it, and even if the kid looked shifty enough for you to wonder what he was up to, you didn't *see* him drop anything on the floor."

Lissa sent Trevor a grateful look. "Quick thinking, to blame the mud on your boots."

An unwilling laugh broke from Viv. "I can still picture it, Trev standing there, scraping all the mouse pellets into a heap under his feet, with the tennis club ladies tut-tutting at him because he hadn't wiped his boots before coming in."

"Anyway," Georgie pointed out, "Now we have the advantage. We know that Jim Beggs is implicated in all of this. We just have to figure out if it's *only* him or if the rest of his little crew are involved as well."

"And we don't know why they're targeting us," Lissa added. "Is it because we're a threat to other businesses or because he wants us out of the building?" She shook her head in impatience. "I'm sure it's simple, in the end."

Outside, thunder rolled again, and the rain pelted down. Georgie's eyes met Scott's, and she knew that he too was thinking of Louise's warning about water damage.

Scott checked his watch. "Maureen will be here for her reading in about fifteen minutes, so let's wrap it up. Georgie, see what else you can get out of her. We want to know if she is involved or has any knowledge of what Jim has been up to."

Georgie nodded, praying that Maureen had nothing to do with it.

"Trev and I have both been up to check the roof of the cafe, inside and out. As far as we can see, it's water-proof, right Trev?"

Trevor nodded. "Ditto for your house. Shouldn't be any concerns about water damage there."

"Moving on to the possibility of another break-in…." Scott picked up the tablet to have a look at the email that Bluey had sent. "Ron Foley is the only one of the four who has been in real trouble for dodgy business practices, so he has to be a suspect. On the other hand, Stan Lambert would probably have a key. We've seen no signs of forced entry. Jim's got to be a possibility, given his behavior today. The dentist?" He shrugged. "Can't find much on him, apart from the fact that he's in a lot of the consortiums that they've set up. Can't rule anyone out, but he's probably the least likely."

Georgie cut in. "We agree we've pretty much ruled out Amber and Shane?" She addressed Trevor, since he was the one still a bit puzzled by it all. "We thought Amber might have been the one to drop the cockroaches, but after seeing the backpacker at work this afternoon, it looks like it's Jim. Getting transients to do his dirty work."

"And we're guessing that last backpacker they had was responsible for the cockroaches," Viv said, a touch of bitterness in her voice. "He's long gone."

"Stan Lambert is also known for something else," Scott said. "Bluey found a few references online from people who have been persuaded to sell for well below market value, only to find that he swoops in and makes a killing. He keeps his nose clean but associates with others who don't mind a dirty trick or two."

He didn't have to say it, but they all knew who he meant – Jim Beggs and Ron Foley.

"A couple more things," Scott said, checking his watch again. "Trev and I are going to be watching the cafe tonight. In case they're watching to see if we go in, we're going to be stationed in the backyard of Linda's shop next door, keeping an eye on things. There's a gate between the two properties, so we can move in quickly if we need to. We can park the LandCruiser there, too, off the street."

"You're going to be drenched," Georgie said, listening to the rain drumming against the roof of the RV.

"We'll live." Scott grinned at her. "Final thing: we've got a few matches for the birthdays that my mother saw when she read the cards." He cast a humorous look at Trev. "All this might sound a bit weird to you, Trev, but the rest of us are used to taking notice of what my mother turns up. She saw two women of significance— one was Aries, the other Taurus. That fits with Maureen and her mother, Vi, who died a few months back. Georgie's got a reading with Maureen tonight, so we think she'll find out more there. The other two… "He exchanged a glance with Georgie. "The other two birthdays match the birthdates of Jim Beggs and Ron Foley."

There was silence for a moment, and Trevor looked a bit stunned before he shrugged and nodded.

"That's about it for now," Georgie said. "Sorry, guys, I'm going to have to kick you all out and go up to the gate to meet Maureen—if she turns up in this weather."

They all stood up and started pulling on raincoats and grabbing umbrellas.

Georgie shook her head at Scott as he prepared to go off with Trevor. "This Australian weather. Bushfires one week, storms the next. You like to challenge a girl, don't you?"

"Just testing you," he said he said, dropping a kiss on

her nose. "Can't be a girly girl to survive in the outback. This is just a taster."

With that, they all slogged up to the gate, holding umbrellas up against the rain, where the rest of them dispersed to their cars just as Maureen pulled up.

Georgie took a deep breath. How was she supposed to break the news that her husband was worth millions?

Subtly, that's how—just a hint for Maureen to follow up.

# 24

# Maureen's Reading

GEORGIE AND MAUREEN ran from the visitor's car park back to the caravan, exchanging rueful grins as the rain beat down in a steady rhythm.

"I wasn't sure whether you'd come," Georgie admitted as they tumbled through the door.

"And I wasn't sure whether you'd want to go ahead with it."

"Scott couldn't stay," Georgie told her, handing her a towel to dry off. "He already had another commitment —but you can come back tomorrow for a card reading if you like."

"I might do that." Maureen looked around her admiringly. "This is lovely. What fun to travel around Australia in this!"

"I'm looking forward to it," Georgie admitted. She kind of hoped the rest of her trip was a little less exciting than the first month, but she wasn't about to tell Maureen that.

Maureen's gaze fell on the quilt, which Georgie had

put back on the bed. "Oh, your quilt! It looks perfect there, doesn't it?"

"It does. And when I go back to the States, I'll have my Australian quilt to remind me of my adventures here." Georgie gestured to the dinette with the crystal ball on the table. "Take a seat. Would you like a hot drink?"

"No, thanks, I'm not cold. Just a bit damp." Maureen sat opposite the crystal ball, her eyes riveted to the shining crystal globe. Georgie already had her LED candle flickering on a little corner shelf, so she flicked off the main light before sitting down.

Immediately, the caravan became cozier, more intimate.

Maureen, unlike many of Georgie's customers, wasn't a bit intimidated by it all. Rather, her eyes were bright with anticipation. "I love this kind of thing. The woman who does the tarot cards at the market is really good; I always go to her for a reading. I can't *wait* to see what comes out of this."

Privately, Georgie thought that the tarot card reader couldn't have been all *that* good since Maureen didn't appear to have any idea of the extent of her husband's betrayal.

"I usually start by asking whether there's anything you'd like to know," Georgie told her. She ran her fingertips over the crystal ball and waited. "You can ask out loud, or you can just hold the question in your mind."

"Oh." Maureen bit her lip while she thought. "It would be kind of nice to be surprised. How about you just tell me what you see, and then I can ask questions later?" She put her fingers to her forehead and closed her eyes tight. "Okay, I'm thinking of a question."

Georgie almost laughed at Maureen's obvious effort to concentrate but choked it back and focused on the crystal ball instead.

She blinked. Right away, a furious grey mist was rising from the depths, swirling angrily.

Wow. It was rare to get such a swift, almost violent reaction.

She tried to relax, to let the messages appear as they would, but it was one of those readings where no images appeared at all.

No audio, no words, either.

Just *information* flooding into her mind.

Georgie took several deep breaths against the onslaught.

Maureen seriously disliked her husband; that was clear. Georgie wouldn't go so far as to say Maureen hated him, but she wanted to change things. To get away from him, as far as possible.

Keeping one hand on the crystal ball, Georgie rested her forehead on the other, letting the impressions flow.

Maureen had had a tough time of it recently. She could feel the other woman's compassion as she nursed her dying mother; could feel that mother's anger channeled through Maureen. Her mother had never liked Jim Beggs, that was clear. And Georgie was sensing some kind of trickery there, too.

No, not trickery. It was more like her mother had been…twisting things.

Twisting things? Setting something up? Georgie concentrated harder and then got an impression of an austere office and people in formal suits. Lawyers? Solicitors?

Oh. Suddenly, she understood, with perfect clarity.

Maureen's mother's *will*. Her mother didn't like Jim Beggs. She had structured her will in a way to ensure that Jim Beggs wouldn't get his hands on her money.

"Georgie?" Maureen's hesitant voice sounded as though it was coming from a distance. "Uh…do you want me to ask a question now?"

Georgie came back to earth with a thump, opening her eyes to find Maureen staring at her. "Sure. If you like."

Maureen darted a glance at the crystal ball, still filled with mist the color of licorice. "Does it always go black and smoky like that?"

"Sometimes." *Hardly ever,* Georgie thought. *Not that dark.*

Suddenly, Maureen spoke, her voice shaky. "What would happen if I divorced Jim? Would he be able to take everything away from me? We've got our house and a little duplex over near the mall and the cafe… but he says there's a lot of debt still on the duplex and the house. He had to re-mortgage the house for a deposit on the duplex. Would I have enough money to live after he pays everything off? I mean, I know you're not an accountant, but… can you see anything?"

Georgie reached over and took her hand. "He can't take it all. Divorce doesn't work that way, Maureen. How long have you been helping Jim? Working in the shop, building up the business?"

Maureen's mouth twisted. "Too long. Nearly a lifetime."

"Then you helped to create everything you own, and you're entitled to a fair share." Georgie squeezed Maureen's cold fingers. "And I have a sense that your mother wanted to protect you, didn't she? She's tied up her money somehow, so Jim can't get to it?"

Maureen's mouth fell open as she stared at Georgie in shock and then at the crystal ball. "Is that what you just saw?"

"Yes." Georgie nodded, holding her gaze. "*Felt* it, more than saw it. I'm sometimes wrong, though. Tell me if I'm wrong."

After a pause, Maureen shook her head. "You're not…goodness; I can't believe you knew that. How could you see that? That's *exactly* what she did."

Georgie already felt drained, and they'd barely started. Somehow she felt that Jim's negative energy was hovering around them both. "What else would you like to know?"

Maureen's gaze dropped to the table, and she played with her watch. "I…well…can you see whether Viv and Lissa will be all right?"

Instantly, Georgie's attention sharpened. Why would Maureen ask that?

Perhaps she *had* been involved in some way with the girls' bad luck.

"I think so," she said slowly, feeling her way. "To be quite honest, they don't feel that everything that has happened to them is an accident. Why do you ask?"

Maureen swallowed and looked miserable. "Because it's partly our fault. Jim dobbed them in them about all the tables on the footpath, on Melbourne Cup day last year. I heard him call Stan Lambert, and then Lambert phoned the girls, and it made all their customers cranky. Everyone was talking about it. I feel really bad. I should have stopped him."

Relieved, Georgie breathed again. "But if it

wasn't *you* who reported them, you weren't to blame."

"I should have stood up to him. Not just about that, about a lot of things." She sighed heavily. "I'm doing it *now*, I'm just starting to, but I wish I'd said something when he did that. It wasn't a nice thing to do."

"It's not your fault," Georgie repeated. Then, softly, she said, "Is that all he's done?"

"No," she said, looking even more woebegone. "When Irene came over after she saw the cockroaches, all huffing and puffing and saying how disgraceful it was, he told her she should report them. She might not have thought of it if it wasn't for him."

Georgie looked at her. Should she take it any further?

"Still," she said, "it was Irene who did that, not you. Perhaps Jim bears some of the responsibility, but unless he actually walked over and let them loose, it wasn't his fault either, I suppose."

She held her breath.

"I guess you're right," Maureen said. "We all know how hard it is to keep on top of cockroaches. I just thought they were unlucky, having a few scuttle around at the wrong time. I was a bit mad at Irene for doing that."

Georgie relaxed. Thank goodness. She *really* hadn't wanted Maureen to be involved in all this. She decided not to tell her about today's incident with Anton and the mouse droppings. Maureen had enough to cope with right now.

The other woman was still sitting there with a faraway look on her face, looking…almost defeated. Georgie could not begin to know what life must be like for her.

Making a decision, she drew the crystal ball toward her. "There's just one more thing, Maureen…from what you've told me, it doesn't make sense, but I'll share it with you anyway."

The other woman looked up, puzzled.

"About Jim…I just have the strongest feeling that he might be a little better off than he's admitting." *Like nearly two million better off.* "I could be mistaken."

"Really?" Maureen frowned, looking skeptical, as her eyes searched Georgie's face.

"It's a possibility. I see three other men involved. Men he sees regularly…does that mean anything to you?"

"Yes," she said immediately. "Stan Lambert, Ron Foley, and Stephen Patterson. Golfing partners. Jim got onto the duplex we own through Stan."

The moment she uttered the name *Ron Foley*, Georgie saw a mental image of Ron's ex-wife, Linda Malloy, so clearly that she might as well have been standing in the same room.

She was standing, nose to nose, with Ron. Arguing, Furious.

*Linda knows something.*

Georgie looked across at Maureen. "I'm getting one message loud and clear, Maureen. It would help if you made the time to talk to Linda Malloy. Things will become clearer, I think."

The angry dark cloud in the crystal ball began to dissipate, and along with it went some of Georgie's tension. Holding Maureen's gaze, she said quietly, "I'd contact Linda sooner rather than later. And maybe not say anything to Jim."

# 25

# In the Wee Small Hours

THEY THOUGHT they were so smart, those Mowbray women.

First Linda, now them. Women messed up everything.

Little did they know that the Mowbray Sisters' Enemy No. 1 was *well* aware that their brother had taken to sleeping on the premises at night. He was sneaky about it, waiting until dark and then making his way there on foot from the caravan park, but he wasn't fooling anyone.

There was a way to fix that little problem. A brother looking out for his sisters was sure to go charging to the rescue if anything happened to them.

That could be arranged.

Feeling almost cheerful, he gave Scott Mowbray a good few hours to settle in at the cafe while he rested at home, dozing and refining his plan. He couldn't see anything wrong with it—in fact, he thought it was excellent. It brought back memories of the fun he and his partner in crime used to have as teenagers.

He'd gone over several different scenarios. What was the most likely thing to make women panic enough to call in the troops? He toyed with the idea of a fire, but that could get out of hand all too quickly, and he was no murderer. He might have spent a few enjoyable hours *imagining* a quick and dirty homicide to get rid of the people he didn't like, but there was a big difference between daydreaming about something like that and doing it.

Besides, the big drawback to committing actual bodily harm was that it could earn him jail time. Did he want that after all these years of managing to avoid it?

No way, José.

He lay there thinking about how it would all play out and discarded a few options after looking at them from different angles. Then he thought of the perfect way to make sure that nobody would discover what he was up to until it was way too late, and smiled at the ceiling.

Step One, Step Two, Step Three.

He would have made a good career criminal if he hadn't decided to stay straight—straight-*ish*—and stuck to making money the easy way.

It was a filthy night, with rain drumming on the roof. A fire wouldn't have worked anyway, he reflected, listening to the downpour.

He briefly considered leaving things for another night or two until the weather improved but then thought again of those wild days back in high school, when he and his friends had discovered that stormy nights were ideal for breaking into cars and houses. The noise of wind and rain covered other sounds, and if anyone *did* hear something, they generally thought twice about investigating if they had to step out into the rain.

More than once, he'd seen a light click on and a face peer out into a dark, wet night, only to disappear again when its owner went back to bed.

He might be decades older, but he hadn't lost his mojo. A bit of rain never hurt anyone.

Two a.m. seemed to take a long, long time to come. He passed the time watching TV—or rather, staring mindlessly at the screen—and then, relieved to be moving, heaved himself off the bed and set about collecting what he needed.

It wouldn't take much.

When he was ready, he backed the car quietly out of the driveway and rolled off down the street in the rain, the wiper blades swishing rhythmically. It wasn't likely that his neighbors would be awake to hear anything at this hour of the morning, even if the storm hadn't masked the sound of his departure.

The other nights, he'd always walked to the girls' cafe, taking care not to be seen. You could always slip behind a tree or duck down behind a car if you were on foot.

Right. Step one, pay a visit to the Mowbray girls' home.

They wouldn't be expecting that.

***

It had taken Lissa a while to get to sleep, mulling over the backpacker's actions and the likely involvement of Jim Beggs, which led her thoughts to Ron Foley and Stan Lambert, which made her angry all over again. Which one had been breaking into the café? Or was it all three? The rain kept her awake, too, worrying about water damage or floods after her mother's warning. It was well after midnight when she finally dropped off.

She was in a deep sleep when a loud crash had her sitting bolt upright in bed, her pulse racing and the sense of terror making her instinctively scrabble backward against the bed head.

*Who? What…?*

Then she heard Viv's voice call out, a note of hysteria rising. "Lissa? *Lissa!?*"

"I'm here," she yelled, launching herself out of bed.

Viv appeared in the doorway, her eyes wide, as she stared at Lissa and then behind her, back into the hallway.

"Did you hear that? What was it?"

"I heard a crash." Lissa shook her head, disoriented. "I don't—what *was* it?"

Viv disappeared, and Lissa could hear her footsteps padding toward the sitting room. She followed her sister, her heart thudding. What now?

She heard the click of a switch, and the sitting room flooded with light, and then Viv held out a hand behind her to stop her. "Stay there, Liss," she ordered, her voice shaky. "There's glass everywhere."

Lissa pushed her aside to peer into the room and gasped. Across the room, the shattered window was letting in the wind and rain, setting the curtains billowing. On the floor lay a house brick, surrounded by gleaming fragments of glass. "A brick? You're kidding. Someone chucked a *brick* through our window?"

Viv sagged against the doorjamb. "I don't believe this. Now someone is attacking us in our *home*."

Before Lissa had a chance to reply, there was a loud thump as something heavy hit the back door. She couldn't prevent a shrill yelp of fear, reaching out for Viv.

Viv swore and whipped around, taking a step in the direction of the door. "Just wait until I—!" her eyes snapped with fury.

"No. No, Viv." Lissa hung onto her arm. "Don't go out; please don't. We haven't got a clue who's out there. They might be trying to force us outside. Just phone Scott."

For a moment, Viv resisted, but then the fire in her eyes muted slightly, and she nodded, moving over to the kitchen counter where their phones were charging.

Lissa heaved herself onto a kitchen stool while she listened to their end of the conversation, feeling a heavy weight grow in her chest.

First the cafe, now their home.

Who could want them out of town this badly?

---

As soon as he heaved the second brick against the back door, the Mowbray Sisters' No. 1 Enemy hurried away, halfway down the street to where he'd left his car neatly tucked away between two others, in a pool of shadow under a dripping tree. Now, all he had to do was watch and make sure their brother turned up to check things out, and then head off to put the second part of his plan into operation.

*Step One, Step Two, Step Three…*

# 26

# Water, Water Everywhere...

JUST TWENTY MINUTES of waiting in Linda Malloy's back yard, under the inadequate protection of a gum tree with branches that creaked ominously in the rain, was enough to convince Scott and Trevor that nobody else was likely to be lurking outside in this weather. A dry night inside the cafe seemed like a much more sensible option.

They let themselves in through the back door, removed their muddy footwear, and toweled off in the bathroom before swiping the towel over the wet tracks they'd left on the floor.

"Nobody's going to be coming out in this," Scott said, standing in the kitchen doorway and peering out at the rain slanting down through the streetlight outside.

"Don't be so sure of that. I had all my tools stolen one night in a thunderstorm." Trevor leaned back on one of the folding chairs Scott had brought around earlier that day, as well as the camp stretcher he'd used to sleep there on other nights. "Who's your money on?"

"Got to be one of three. Jim Beggs, Ron Foley, or

Stan Lambert. Don't think it's the dentist." Scott went back and sat in the other chair.

"My conclusion too." Trev folded his hands across his stomach, his face dim in the muted glow from the LED readouts on various electrical appliances. "My gut tells me that it's not Stan. He's Mr. Clean, on the council and all that. He might know about it, but he wouldn't be taking risks."

Scott nodded. He'd been thinking the same way. "Ron's played dirty games in the past to get what he wants. From what my brother managed to dig up, this smells of him."

"Don't discount Jim. He might look ten years older, but they're the same age, went to school together. Trouble all the way, from what I heard."

"And he was behind today's little game, and probably the cockroaches too."

"But he got backpackers to do it," Trev pointed out. "Like Stan, it seems he's decided it's better to let others get their hands dirty. If the three of them are teaming up on this one, he might be leaving it to Ron to handle the risky stuff."

Scott stretched his arms above his head, linked his fingers, and cracked his knuckles, swallowing a yawn. If it hadn't been for his mother's conviction that there was some threat from water, he'd be tempted to go back to the caravan and get a good night's sleep in a decent bed. The last couple of nights here had been restless and uncomfortable.

"You want to grab some sleep? I can do the first stint," Trev offered.

"A bit early yet." Despite his words, Scott yawned again. "What I can't figure out is *why*. If Stan wants the girls out of the restaurant, why doesn't he just pay out the lease?"

Trev laughed caustically. "Anyone around town will tell you that both Stan and Jim make Scrooge look good. If they can avoid paying out a lease, they will. More than likely, they've extended themselves too far, and there's no cash flow. Their thinking would be that it's easier to drive them out."

"I was there when Lambert offered them a deal on commercial premises over near the mall. Fifty percent of the rent for the first four months."

"Yeah, Viv told me about that. They're empty; he's having trouble getting tenants. Half rent for four months is better than zero. And if it gets them out of here, he's laughing." Trev was silent for a moment, then added, "My guess is that Stan and the others are on some kind of deadline. Big money to be made later, but not much in the short term."

"I thought they were all worth millions."

"On paper, maybe. You know how it is with these blokes. They over-invest, and then the whole thing collapses."

Outside, the rain increased in intensity and battered against the kitchen window for ten minutes before easing up and settling into steady drumming.

"At this rate," Scott said, "it won't be a leak from the roof the girls have to worry about; it'll be flood damage. The gutters are overflowing out there."

"I think they'll be right. They're up a bit from street level."

They talked for a while, about Yamba and its inhabitants and Trev's business, until ten o'clock when Trev took the first watch while Scott drifted into a half-sleep on the camp stretcher. At one a.m., they swapped over.

Just after two-thirty, Scott's phone rang, cutting through the sound of the rain. He jerked upright in the chair, ready for trouble. "Hello?"

He listened, tight-lipped, while Trev, instantly awake, sat up and swung his feet onto the floor.

"We're on our way," Scott said, on his feet and grabbing his jacket. He shoved his phone in his pocket. "It's the girls. Someone's just tossed a brick through their window."

---

Jim Beggs watched Scott Mowbray's LandCruiser flash past him and park outside his sisters' house. Two figures got out and hurried up to the front door.

*Two* men. That was interesting. He couldn't make out who they were from half a street away, with the windscreen fogged up and rain still drifting down, but it seemed Mowbray had decided to bring in reinforcements.

Which didn't matter at all, seeing they were here, exactly where he wanted them to be, and not at the cafe.

He pulled out of his parking space, did a U-turn, and drove away.

The rain both complicated things and made them easier. There was no way to avoid getting wet since he planned to park his car out of sight at the back of his place of business and walk to the cafe, but the rain also meant that nobody with half a brain would be out in it.

Sure enough, the streets were deserted, and by the

time he reached the back door of *Coffee, Cakes & Crepes*, he hadn't seen a soul.

His first action was to turn the water off at the mains. Once that was accomplished, he let himself in and headed straight to the kitchen, where he immediately fell over a camp chair in the gloom.

With a curse, he kicked it over, then thought twice and picked it up again. If he had figured it right, they'd be back. An overturned camp chair would be a sure sign of an intruder.

Moving over to the dishwasher, he pulled a small battery-powered lantern from his pocket, switched it to half-power, and set it on the floor, so he could see what he was doing.

It didn't take long to pull the dishwasher out and slit the hose at the back. Simple but effective. He slid the appliance back in again and then shone the lantern around to make sure he hadn't left any trace of his visit. He bit back a curse when he saw his muddy footprints.

Damn rain.

Crossing the room, he tore off a dozen sheets of paper toweling on a wall dispenser and mopped up the evidence before crumpling up the paper and shoving it in his pocket.

Job done. Step Two accomplished.

Almost finished. He'd hang about until Mowbray came back to check on things, wait until he left again, then turn the water back on at the mains and go home while the split hose did its work. If Mowbray *didn't* come back, that would mean a re-think, but he was confident he'd turn up. They'd all be running scared, not knowing what was going to happen next.

He pulled up the hood of his waterproof jacket and

stepped outside, locking the door behind him before slipping through the gate that led into the backyard of Linda Malloy's shop next door.

Mowbray should give the place a quick once-over, see that nothing looked out of place, and then leave again to be with his sisters.

Or the police.

Or both. However it played out, Mowbray would be well and truly occupied while his sisters' cafe slowly flooded.

Luckily the rain had finally eased, so the wait wasn't as miserable as it might have been.

The Mowbray Sisters' No. 1 Enemy settled down to wait.

---

27

# End Play

---

WHEN SCOTT ARRIVED, Lissa flung the door open and went straight to her brother for a hug. "I'm so glad you're here. Oh, Scotty…"

He could feel her trembling in his arms, his feisty, take-no-prisoners little sister. All of this had worn her down. He kissed the top of her head, rubbed her back, and made a conscious effort to quash his anger, to give her the calmness she needed.

Over her shoulder, he saw Trev put an arm around Viv, which made her face crumple as she turned to put her head on his chest. His eyes met Trev's, and he read the message there: this was where it was going to end. Somehow, they'd follow this through, confront Foley and Beggs and Lambert, face them down. Threaten them with an investigation—armed with the information that his brother had uncovered.

During the next half hour, Viv and Lissa got over the first shock and started getting angry again. Scott took photos of the damage and called the police to report it, only to find they were all out attending to car accidents and local flooding.

It was when Lissa said for what seemed like the hundredth time, "Which one? Which *one?* And why attack us here?" that it suddenly hit Scott.

"Oh hell," he said, jumping to his feet. "The cafe."

Trev took about two seconds to follow his thoughts. "Bugger."

It dawned on his sisters at the same time.

"They *wanted* you here," Lissa said. "Out of the cafe." She seemed to shrink, not wanting to face whatever else might have been done.

"A diversion." Scott strode through to the laundry to grab their damp jackets and came back, tossing Trev his. "We'll have to check it out." He paused, irresolute. "Will you girls be right here, or do you want to go hang out with Georgie?"

"We're coming with you," Lissa said, in a tone that brooked no argument.

Scott was happy enough with that. He didn't fancy leaving them alone in a house with a broken window, with nothing more than a tarp over it to keep out the rain.

Or intruders.

Within minutes, they were pulling up outside the cafe, Scott no longer troubling to keep his movements secret. He didn't even bother suggesting that his sisters wait in the car. If there was any damage, they'd want to know immediately.

Viv unlocked the front door, flicked a switch to illuminate the main dining area, then immediately huffed out a sigh of relief.

It all looked undisturbed.

She and Lissa exchanged a look and moved quickly to the kitchen, followed by Scott and Trev. Another light switch clicked, and they all stared around.

They saw nothing but the camp chairs and the single stretcher brought in by Scott earlier. The benches were clean and shining, the appliances all hummed as they should, and there was nobody there who shouldn't have been.

Scott glanced up at the ceiling, just in case, but there were no leaks.

He huffed out a huge sigh of relief. "Nothing to worry about, it seems. I'll check out back, just in case."

A quick look outside showed only dripping trees and a deserted two-space parking area. Everything looked tidy and undisturbed.

He locked the back door and returned. "Nothing."

"So the broken window was just to scare us." Viv's earlier anger had given way to a look of defeat. The roller-coaster emotions she had experienced over the past few hours were beginning to tell. "Wearing us down."

Scott hugged her again. "Come on. Let's get you home; think about what to do next."

She just nodded, looking weary.

"Viv." He put a finger under her chin and tipped it up. "We *will* end this. Somehow. The backpacker today, the brick tonight…it's all gone way too far."

She managed a tired smile. "So this is war?"

"You bet. It's *Mowbray* war."

That reference to their childhood games made her smile. "All right."

Scott looked over at Trevor. "Trev? Do you want me

to drop you home? You should be able to catch a few hours' sleep before you have to get up for work."

"I'll hang at the girls' place for a while," Trevor said. "My jobs will all be canceled anyway, with the rain. You'll need to get back to Georgie, and the girls will have to open the cafe. I'll stay at their place until the window is repaired." He glanced at Viv. "If that's okay with you."

"That's so good of you, Trev." Viv sent him a weak smile. "I was wondering what we'd do."

They left the cafe and piled back into the car. It looked like their long night was just about over.

---

Satisfied, Jim Beggs listened until the sound of the LandCruiser died away in the distance and came out of hiding to execute Step Three.

It all worked like a charm; it couldn't have been easier. Walk to the water mains, turn the water back on, job done.

He returned to his car and drove home.

When the Mowbray women turned up to open the cafe in the morning, they'd be greeted by a small inland sea.

———————————

28

# Caught

———————————

MAUREEN BEGGS KNEW that her husband had a shady past. She'd been unaware of it when she first married Jim, who seemed to be honest and hard-working if a bit of a rough diamond. Then one day, when the children were small, she overheard Jim and Ron laughing about how they used to go joyriding in stolen cars and do a few break-and-enters for ready cash.

When Jim realized she'd heard, he dismissed it as youthful folly. Lots of teenage boys sowed wild oats, he told her. As long as you straightened yourself out and became a good citizen, that's all that counted.

At the time, Maureen had believed him, but Jim had gradually changed from a hard-working man of a few words to one who was taciturn and penny-pinching and finally into a grumpy, cheerless old man.

After seeing Georgie, she was now certain that one kind of stealing had merely given way to another. Jim just interpreted the law to suit himself when it came to investments and property.

He was stealing from *her*.

For the first time, she had an inkling of what he'd been up to throughout their marriage. All these years, when he'd let her think that he was just working hard for *them*, he was looking after his own interests.

He'd probably planned on divorcing her anyway, once he didn't need her anymore.

When she returned from her reading with Georgie, she was sorely tempted to go and confront Jim in the bedroom he'd set up for himself, with its little attached sitting room, but told herself to be patient. First, Linda Malloy. She couldn't wait until the next day. Not with all this buzzing around in her head.

Shutting herself in her bedroom, she found Linda's number on her phone and rang her.

"Hello, Linda," she said, nervous but angry. "It's Maureen. I—"

Before she got another word out, Linda said, "I was wondering when you'd call. I think we have a lot to talk about."

When they finished talking, forty minutes later, Maureen was angrier than she'd ever been and filled with a new determination to make Jim pay. Linda had promised to call her divorce lawyer and make an appointment for Maureen the very next day.

Satisfying though that prospect was, Maureen found sleep elusive. She heard Jim walking from his bedroom to the kitchen, then back to his bedroom, and finally the muted sound of a television in his sitting room, on the other side of her bedroom wall.

He never usually watched TV this late.

He was probably mad at her for leaving him in the cafe by himself today while she went to the quilting group. Although she hadn't left him in the lurch, had she? She'd made sure that Anton was available.

She reflected that Anton had better be available for a lot more shifts now. She knew she couldn't stomach working alongside Jim for another day, now that she knew what she knew.

Finally, the sound of the TV stopped. *At last*, thought Maureen. She had enough trouble getting to sleep without that.

Then Jim's door opened and closed softly, and she heard him tiptoeing past her door. There was just the faintest hint of a footfall.

Maureen frowned and looked at the digital readout on the clock beside her. Why was Jim creeping about at two o'clock in the morning?

Painfully aware that her husband was proving to be someone she didn't know at all, she got out of bed and, holding her breath, eased open the door of her bedroom and stole down the hallway to where it opened into the living room—just in time to hear the click of the door between the kitchen and the garage as it closed. She barely caught it because of the rain on the roof.

Straining her ears, she heard the side door to the garage close softly. Jim was going *outside*, in this weather?

Hastening to the window overlooking the street, she watched in astonishment as Jim got into the car, shutting the door as quietly as he was doing everything else, and backed out of the driveway, the sound of his departure masked by the rain.

He didn't switch on the headlights until he was clear of the house.

She had no idea where Jim Beggs, her husband of over forty years, was going at two o'clock in the morning in the pouring rain. She *was* certain that he was up to no good.

Her mind instantly flew to *Coffee, Cakes & Crepes,* and she shivered.

If anything bad happened tonight, she knew who they should be looking at.

***

Maureen wasn't the only one who couldn't sleep. The sound of rain was always amplified in an RV, and the rain had been falling steadily for hours and hours, drumming on the roof, splattering against the windows.

After staring at the ceiling for far too long, Georgie slipped out of bed and made herself a cup of Earl Grey, even though caffeine at three o'clock in the morning wasn't the best idea. Chamomile would probably have been a more sensible choice.

She didn't even make a conscious decision to consult the crystal ball. On autopilot, she set the cup down on the table, reached for the crystal ball, and slid off the black velvet cloth that covered it.

*Something's wrong.* She knew it; as surely as she knew her name was Georgina Bridget Goode.

That was probably why the familiar mist in the crystal ball formed in seconds, and images quickly followed.

The first face she saw was Viv, looking afraid, and then Viv and Lissa together. Lissa seemed to be imploring her sister, holding her back.

Rain. Rain inside their house, wetting the sofa—she could see a damp stain spreading.

Thrusting down a sharp sense of panic, Georgie deliberately drew in several deep, calming breaths. Scott's mother had been right, but *how*? Scott and Trev had checked out the roof of both the house and the cafe.

Georgie peered closer, opening her mind. Was she seeing what she *expected* to see, or what had happened?

Or maybe what was *going* to happen?

The scene changed, and she was looking at water spreading again. A widening pool of water, sliding across the floor, lapping at the sofa again.

No, no. This wasn't the same sofa, and the floor was tiled, not carpeted.

This time, she realized, she was looking at the big squashy dusky pink sofa in the cafe.

The scene blinked out, and the mist filled the crystal ball. For a couple of seconds, Maureen Beggs' face filled the center of the ball. Maureen, looking madder than Georgie had ever seen her.

Then nothing.

Georgie looked at her watch.

Three-fifteen.

Something was *so* wrong.

After they returned from the cafe, Scott was just accepting a cup of coffee from Lissa when the phone rang, the lilting tune that he'd set for Georgie.

He wasn't surprised. If anyone could sense that something was wrong, it would be Georgie.

Scott put her on speaker so everyone could hear. "Hey, Georgie."

"Scott, I'm seeing water in the girls' house," she said. "A wet sofa. And—"

"They got a brick through the window," he said. "About two this morning. Trev and I came right over. They're listening to you now."

"We're okay," Viv called from the stool at the kitchen counter.

"That's good," she said. "But listen, guys…it's not just the house. You need to go and check the cafe, too. I saw *both*. Water everywhere."

Scott looked at Trev sitting beside him, and he could feel the tension emanating from his sisters. "Trev and I spent most of the night at the cafe, Georgie. No water coming in—and we've not long come back from there, just in case the brick was a ruse to get us to leave. It was fine."

They all heard an intake of breath on the other end of the phone, and then Georgie's voice, firm and sure. "No. It's *not* fine. You need to go back, Scott, now. I saw water spreading right across the floor. Your mother was right."

"All right." Without hesitation, he put his coffee mug down and stood up. "I'll do it now and call you back."

"Wait, Scott—are you still there?"

"Yes."

"You should check on Maureen, too. I don't know why, but you should. Tell her I was worried about her."

"I will. Cafe first, then Maureen."

He knew better than to suggest that his sisters stay behind.

They drove back again and parked again in front of the cafe. Back through the front door.

This time, the moment the light went on, it was clear that everything was far from fine.

Water was spilling through the kitchen door and spreading quickly across the tiled cafe floor. As they stared in horror, it reached the sofa, and the first dark water stain started wicking upward.

"The mains," said Trevor, splashing through to the back door. "Scott, key!"

Scott tossed him the keys and headed straight for the kitchen. One glance showed him that the water was streaming out from under the dishwasher.

Behind him, Viv and Lissa were grabbing towels from the bathroom and tablecloths from a cupboard, racing back to protect the sofa from the water.

For the second time that night, they all worked together to clean up water damage. Again, Scott phoned the police. He wasn't positive that this was a crime scene, but he was sure enough to forbid anyone to touch the dishwasher, just in case there were prints on it.

Grim-faced, Viv took photos for the insurance company.

Nobody said much; they all just worked. It was almost as though there was nothing left that could shock them.

Once the tide had been stemmed, Scott phoned Georgie back. "You were right—water all over the floor. You wouldn't believe how much this spread just in the time we were away. Whoever it was must have been waiting and watching, then came in the minute we left."

"I've been thinking about that," Trev said, hearing him. "Would have been simple enough to set it up while we were at the house after the brick came through the window. Then just turn the mains off. They guessed we'd be back."

Scott looked at him, instantly seeing it. "I think you're on to something there."

Lissa's eyes flashed in fury. "When you left the second time, they'd bank on us not returning until morning." She pointed to the back door. "Do you think he left footprints? It's so wet out there."

"Could be. We'll leave that up to the police." Scott returned his attention to the phone. "Give me half an hour, Georgie, and I'll be back. Trev's going to stay with the girls."

"Good. But first—"

"I know," he said. "Check on Maureen. I hadn't forgotten."

"I'll text through her phone number," Georgie said. "Try that first."

## 29

# A New Dawn

AFTER WATCHING JIM SNEAK AWAY, Maureen didn't go back to bed. She sat by the window, watching as the rain eased to a drizzle and then to intermittent showers, thinking about a wasted life.

How could she have been so blind?

How could she have been so *weak!*

Her eyelids grew heavy, and when at last the flash of headlights in the driveway made her jerk upright, she realized she had been dozing. A glance at her watch showed that it was 3.41.

Jim had left at two. Where had he been for more than an hour and a half on a wet, miserable night?

She got up and slipped back through the dark rooms to her bedroom, closed the door, and got back into bed, listening.

Ten minutes later, Jim crept past her door and went into his own room. If she hadn't been listening, her awareness extended; it was unlikely she would have heard him.

Maureen lay still, worrying. Whatever he was involved in, she hoped it wouldn't come back on her.

About an hour after Jim returned, her phone suddenly rang, the initial muted one-two beat.

Wide awake, Maureen snatched it up before it got louder and longer. Her fingers were shaking.

"H-hello?"

"Maureen? It's Scott Mowbray. I'm sorry to disturb you at this hour." His voice was calm, reassuring. "Georgie wanted me to phone you and check that you're okay."

Maureen's pulse slowed a little. He didn't sound mad. Maybe nothing had happened.

"I'm all right," she said, but she wasn't even convincing herself. She could hear the wobble in her voice. "I'm…no, I'm not all right, not really. But I don't know what to do."

Scott said immediately, "We're right outside, Maureen. I've got Viv and Lissa with me. Would you like us to come in? Or you could come out to us if you'd rather Jim didn't know."

Maureen couldn't stop the tears sliding down her face. "Did anything happen tonight?"

He hesitated a beat, then said, "Yes. Yes, it did, but everyone's all right, and it's nothing that can't be fixed." His voice was so gentle it made the tears come faster. "Don't you worry."

"I'm coming out," she said in a small voice. "Can you wait a few minutes?"

"We'll wait as long as it takes. Should we come to the door?"

"No. I'll be fine. I'm coming now."

Maureen got out of bed, turned on the light, and

broke all previous records for getting dressed. She threw her phone and wallet in a handbag and eased the door open, almost expecting Jim to be waiting on the other side, barring her way.

The house was silent.

No doubt he was exhausted after being out half the night.

She wished him well cooking his fish and chips today because one thing was for sure: it wasn't going to be *her* doing it.

Maureen walked out of the front door, down the driveway, and was met with a hug from an exhausted-looking Lissa, who was leaning on the car waiting for her.

She didn't deserve those girls to be so nice to her, because if they were outside her house at five in the morning, looking like they'd been through the wringer, she just knew that it was Jim Beggs who was behind it all.

Yet again, *Coffee, Cakes & Crepes* didn't open its doors that day. This time, nobody in the town batted an eyelid, because theirs wasn't the only business in the town with a notice on the door saying *Closed due to Storm Damage.*

Fortunately, there wasn't a great deal of damage, thanks to Georgie's timely alert. Trev replaced the hose on the dishwasher before heading back to the girls' house to secure the broken window, and they'd saved the sofa from anything but a token wetting. Trev took Maureen with him to get some rest and privacy in Viv's guest room.

Meanwhile, Georgie, Scott, and his sisters were busy. Scott had a long conversation with Bluey and got him to email through some very interesting facts and figures on The Gang of Four, as they'd started calling Jim and his golf buddies.

"Just remember," Bluey had said to Scott, serious for a moment, "you didn't get this information from me. Even the Australian Tax Department doesn't have it, although I imagine they'd love to get their hands on it."

"They may get an anonymous tip," Scott said, "but not until we've sorted things out here. Thanks, Bro."

"No worries," Bluey said breezily. "My rates have just doubled."

"You're worth more." Scott grinned at the others. "We'll triple it."

"Can't afford the tax," Bluey said. "Call me if you need more, but I won't be able to get to it until tonight. Because, you know, I have this *real* job?"

"Jury's out on that one. Mum is still convinced you are a super-hacker."

"Never say that on an open line. I deny everything." Bluey terminated the call.

"You don't really pay him to investigate for you, do you?" Lissa asked.

"Of course not. He's a bonafide member of the Crystal Ball Investigation Team. It's all pro bono." Scott sent the pages from Bluey to the wireless printer in the cafe's kitchen and summarized the content for the others. "Next step," he said, "a meeting with Maureen and Linda before we have a little chat with Jim. After that, we'll tackle Ron Foley and Stan Lambert."

At three o'clock that afternoon, Scott located the backpacker's hostel. He parked outside and then suddenly realized what he was looking at. He stood back and took it in, and snapped a photo with his phone to show Georgie.

Outside the building was a table with an umbrella, and the top quarter of the facade was painted orange. It was, he was certain, the building Georgie had seen in the crystal ball days ago.

He shook his head, impressed as always by just how accurate Georgie could be with her gift. It might have helped to realize earlier that backpackers were involved—but it had all played out well enough, in the end.

Better, maybe, because seeing Anton trying to create another health scare had given them more ammunition.

He found Anton lazing around the pool and had a quiet word about mouse droppings, criminal mischief, and termination of his Australian Visa. He quoted legal ramifications that had no basis in reality, but Anton didn't know that. No longer cocky, he agreed to go with them while they talked to Jim.

Scott didn't waste time. He picked up Georgie and Maureen, and then the four of them went to see Jim Beggs, confronting him in the kitchen.

Standing at the kitchen counter with bowls lined up in front of him, looking tired and decidedly cranky, Jim scowled at them. "Bit late for work, aren't you, Maureen?"

Just as tired and completely over Jim's nonsense, Maureen said, "Jim, be quiet and listen," and looked at Scott.

"We know you were behind the flooding of the cafe last night," Scott said, with a nod across the road.

"Maureen will testify that you left the house last night at approximately two in the morning and didn't return until just before a quarter to four."

"If anything happened over there, it's got nothing to do with me," Jim said, his eyes growing hard and his chin jutting belligerently.

"Then there's a little matter of a house brick through my sisters' window. You wouldn't know anything about that, would you?"

"No, I wouldn't."

"Let me lay this on the line for you, Jim. My sisters have been subjected to a string of bad luck for months now. So much so that it is starting to look like a little more than bad luck."

"Not my fault."

"Cockroaches?" Scott pointed at Anton. "Mouse droppings? Reports to the council about too many tables on the footpath?"

Jim's eyes immediately found Maureen's, and his eyebrows lowered further while he glared.

"Yes," she said, "I told them that was you, on Melbourne Cup day."

"My sisters told me that you showed them through when they were looking for premises for the café," Scott said. "I'm assuming you kept the key. And if you had access to interfere with the dishwasher, you could undoubtedly engineer some of the other things that went wrong. Either you or your mate, Ron Foley."

"You're not going to be able to prove any of that."

"We'll be dusting the dishwasher for fingerprints. I believe yours are on file."

Jim's lips tightened as he gazed belligerently at Scott. "Go right ahead."

"We also have Anton's testimony. And we have this." Scott reached into his pocket and withdrew a piece of paper, which he unfolded and handed to Jim. "A list of some of your assets. I'm sure there are more, but these are all we had time to find in the time available."

Jim snatched the paper from him and scanned the list. When he finished, he crumpled it up and then took a step toward Maureen. "You're behind this. All the years I worked, and—"

"No," Scott said, putting out a hand and moving Maureen behind him. "No more intimidation. Facts are facts, Jim. We'll be meeting with Ron and Stan within the hour. You're welcome to attend if you wish, in Stan's office. Call him."

Finally, Jim stopped pretending innocence. "What are you? Some kind of private detective?"

"No. Just someone with contacts." Scott sent him a smile completely devoid of humor. "We're going to have a proposal ready for the three of you. If you want to come out of this with anything but a prison sentence— either for criminal mischief or tax fraud or both—I suggest you listen."

His work done, Scott took Maureen by the arm and left.

---

30

Sunshine

---

IF LOOKS COULD KILL, Georgie thought, she and Scott would have been dead ten times over.

Five of them crowded around the small circular table in the corner of Stan Lambert's office. The men were silently reading through the single page that Scott had handed to each one of them.

One page was enough to make them all glance at each other in trepidation; a sheet of paper that contained a summary of business activities they had thought were well hidden.

Stan Lambert, masking his shock well after the first knee-jerk reaction, was expressionless except for the cold dislike in his eyes. Ron Foley was the loudest, swearing and throwing the sheet of paper down before picking it up to read through it again, every so often stopping to glare at them. Jim Beggs sat there and stewed, his arms folded tightly.

Finally, Stan put the sheet of paper down, aligning it carefully with the edge of his desk. "Where did you get this information?"

"That," Scott said, "I am not prepared to divulge."

"All right. What do you want?"

Foley shoved his chair back from the table, looking ready to pounce. "You're not going to——"

"Ron, don't say a word. Let me handle this." All Stan had to do was stare him down, and Ron subsided with a bit of muttering to save face. Stan's gaze settled on Scott's face, after a glance at Georgie that dismissed her as of no account. "What is your intention?"

"My intention," Scott said, "is to ensure that the Australian Tax Office is anonymously notified of all these transactions, as well as some of the parties that were conned into parting with property for a price significantly under market value." He paused, while Stan again held up a hand to quieten Ron Foley, and then added, "*Unless* you are prepared to compensate certain people."

There was a slight flicker of relief in Stan Lambert's eyes, quickly hidden. This kind of negotiation, he understood. "Go on."

"How can you trust him to do what he says?" Foley burst out. "How do we know that he won't turn us in anyway?"

Lambert sighed. "First, we listen. Then we decide." His eyes hadn't left Scott's.

"First, you can forget about the deal that includes the sale of the property currently being leased by Linda Malloy and my sisters. That isn't going to happen."

That got a reaction from all of them. As Scott's brother had discovered, the sale and demolition of that building was a major factor in a planned development. The Gang of Four all had a finger in that pie.

"We're in too deep." Ron Foley waved it aside, fuming.

"Too late," agreed Jim Beggs.

Stan Lambert said, "You can't stop it now."

"We can and will. If you had offered to buy out the lease," Scott said, keeping calm, "or made a real effort to relocate the cafe in decent premises in the township, it wouldn't have played out this way. But when you took on my sisters, you took on me." He tapped the sheets of information in front of him. "And as I said, I have contacts." He shot Georgie a quick look, and she managed to hide a smile. While the men around the table might fear a hacker like Scott's brother, it's unlikely they would have considered a gypsy fortune-teller a threat. "Once you resort to criminal activity to ruin someone's business and force them out, you have to face the consequences."

"We need that building." Stan Lambert was not giving in easily. "We've agreed—"

"I know exactly where the negotiations stand," Scott said. "I think you'll find that the major player is getting cold feet."

"You're bluffing."

Scott pointed at the phone on Lambert's desk. "Contact Mr. Chang and see what he says. I'll wait."

At the sound of the developer's name, Lambert blanched. "What have you done?"

"Let's cut to the chase. I know that you're in a precarious position with investments, loans, and prop-erty taxes. All of you." Scott looked at each one of them. "You stood to make a killing, but only if things went well. I imagine that's why you were reluctant to pay out the lease for both Linda Malloy and my sisters;

you're stretched way too thin. If I now make this public —any of it—then you're all sunk. You're looking at financial ruin and perhaps a prison term."

Foley turned on Jim. "This is all your fault. I'd just about convinced Linda, offering her a deal to get out. We could have talked the other women into it too. But no, you had to take it too far."

"You thought it was amusing enough when I start-ed," Jim shot back. "Egged me on, didn't you?" He turned his angry gaze on Scott. "And if your sisters hadn't thought they were better than everyone else, bringing in all that fancy stuff, taking my customers, they might not have brought this on themselves."

"Jim," Lambert said in an icy tone, "not another word. No admission of culpability. You *want* prison?"

This time it was Scott's turn to hold up a hand. Georgie could see that he'd had enough of these men. "You can blame each other later," he said. "I'll just tell you the conditions. They're fairer than you deserve, and they're non-negotiable. You agree, and you get to lick your wounds and fight another day. You make trouble, and you're gone."

Stan Lambert tapped the paper in front of him. "Why don't you just go ahead and report this anyway?"

"Because I want my sisters to be able to get on with their lives, not to be subject to court cases and legal proceedings for years. That's the only reason you're getting off lightly."

Stan sat back and mirrored the body language of his friends, folding his arms and waiting.

"All right, we'll talk about the tenancy. What else do you want?"

Scott told them what they wanted for his sisters,

Maureen Beggs, and Linda Malloy, handing each of them another sheet of paper with his demands.

A great deal of name-calling and shouting ensued, but forty-five minutes later, he knew he had won.

By then, Stan Lambert was livid but controlling it. Scott had a feeling that he would be drawing back from investments with the Gang of Four in the future.

Ron Foley broke a chair in a dramatic exit, but they knew that Linda would get something at least approaching a fair share of what was left of his investments after he'd sold off some profitable properties.

Jim Beggs was in a similar situation. There'd be some forced sales in his immediate future, but Maureen would never have to worry about money again—or work in her husband's fish and chip shop.

Georgie and Scott left, drained but triumphant. They couldn't wait to break the news that *Coffee, Cakes, and Crepes* now had a new landlord, thanks to the title of the building being transferred to Linda Malloy. Scott was happy to let Ron Foley and Stan Lambert work that one out between themselves.

That afternoon, at five o'clock, there was a celebration at *Coffee, Cakes & Crepes.* In the space of twenty-four hours, emotions had run the full gamut. Georgie couldn't keep the smile off her face, watching them all.

Lissa and Viv talked non-stop, unable to believe how things had played out, while Scott and Trev just smiled quietly, enjoying their happiness.

Linda closed her shop half an hour early and entered with Maureen in tow. They'd had a lot to talk about, involving hidden properties and divorce proceedings.

The moment she saw Linda, Lissa pounced on her. "Our new landlord! How exciting!" She gave her an exuberant hug. "Bit of an improvement on the last one!"

Linda laughed, freeing herself to hug Viv too, and turned to Scott. "Did you tell them about the lease?"

"No." He grinned at her conspiratorially. "I thought I'd leave that for you."

"What?" Lissa put her hands on her hips and cocked her head, still smiling. "You mean there's more?"

Linda nodded. "I'm extending your lease by three years, with an exit clause if you want to move to different premises. The first six months are rent-free, to compensate you for criminal damage, lost business, and loss of goodwill."

Viv's hand went to her mouth. "Really? But that doesn't seem fair. It wasn't your fault that—"

Linda stopped her with a chuckle. "Don't worry, Lissa. *I'm* not the one paying for it."

Maureen came up to Georgie. "Georgie."

Georgie put a hand on her arm. Maureen looked tired but content. "You okay?"

"I'm fine. It's all been a bit of a shock, and I still feel guilty about what Jim did to the girls."

When Georgie shook her head and started to speak, Maureen stopped her. "No, I have to bear some of the blame. I knew what was right and what wasn't, and I'm sorry for that. But you and the girls—and Scott—you've all been so good to me, better than I deserve. So thanks." She sighed. "Thanks doesn't seem enough."

Georgie pointed to Lissa and Viv. "Look at them.

Everything has worked out just fine. Better than it would have before. It was a rocky road, but in the end, it was a good result, don't you think?"

Maureen conceded the point. "When you put it like that. And when I think of how my life might have turned out, if I'd just stayed with Jim and put up with it…." She shuddered.

"Come on." Georgie nodded to where Linda was popping the cork on a bottle of champagne. "Let's join them."

A good result, indeed, she thought, as she and Scott clinked glasses. She smiled around at the happy faces around her. "Here's to a happy life ahead. And to the next adventure on our trip around Australia. Maybe our next stop will be a bit quieter?"

Scott just laughed. "I wouldn't bet on it, Georgie. But would you have it any other way?"

No, she thought wryly. No, she wouldn't. Life was for living, and she was certainly living it to the full.

*The next book in the Australian Adventure Series…*

## No Good Reason

**A spoilt rich kid hell-bent on revenge.
A good man about to give up on his dream.
And in the background, a secret that could
destroy a family…**

It sounded like a good plan to Georgie and Scott: a few days kayaking around the peaceful waters of St. Georges Basin, followed by relaxed happy hours around the campfire.

But if there is one thing that Georgie has learned, it's that real life tends to laugh at her plans.

A morning's paddle along the canals of Sussex Inlet leads her to Chris Moore, an embattled small business owner who can't see a way out. He is ready to give up—but his wife, Allie, wants him to fight. When she finds out that Georgie is more than a sideshow fortune-teller, she pleads for help.

Georgie and Scott, aided by some cryptic insights from Georgie's crystal ball, begin to tug at threads—and when it all starts to unravel, stumble across secrets that powerful people don't want exposed.

**And one of those secrets could make their new clients wish they'd never asked for help…**

# From the Author

Yamba, where Viv and Lissa live, is lovely part of Australia, on the coast of NSW. If you haven't yet had a chance to visit, I'd put it on your list! Stay for a while, hire a kayak and paddle around, or catch the ferry between Yamba and Iluka (You might even be able to book a Sunday music cruise!) There are some lovely little cafes and restaurants in Yamba, but you won't find *Coffee, Cakes and Crêpes*, since it's entirely a product of my imagination—as is the 'Gang of Four'!

The next book in the series takes Georgie and Scott further down south, to St Georges Basin. She just can't stay out of trouble!

**Have you read Rosa's story yet?**

Join my newsletter subscribers and download this free ebook. You'll find out more about Georgie and her family...and see where she got her special gift!

MargMcAlister.com/free-georgie-book/

I also like to write to my readers with snippets of upcoming books and inside information about Georgie's world!

## ABOUT THE AUTHOR

Marg McAlister is the author of the popular Georgie B. Goode Cozy Mystery series (set in the USA) and Series 2 (Australian RV Adventure series), also featuring Georgie.

Marg lives by the sea on the mid-north coast of NSW, but she and her husband spend part of the year on The Gemfields in Central Queensland, living off the grid on their mining claim. While her husband digs for sapphires and zircons, operates the wash plant and drives around dirt tracks, Marg is usually writing—or socializing!

Marg is also the author of a series of books for aspiring writers, and the owner of Blue Gem Publishing, which publishes books in a range of genres.

## Glossary

Georgie is swiftly becoming accustomed to the way Australians speak, but sometimes people from other countries can be scratching their heads at Australian idioms and contractions. So here's a translation for you of some of the common terms used in this book!

**Ambo** — ambulance officer, paramedic

**Air con** — air conditioning

**Arvo** — afternoon

**Australian States and Territories:**

*QLD* — Queensland

*NSW* — New South Wales

*VIC* — Victoria

*TAS* (or "Tassie") — Tasmania

*SA* — South Australia

*WA* — Western Australia

*NT* — Northern Territory

*ACT* — Australian Capital Territory (in NSW)

**Aussie, Oz** — shortened form of Australia

**back-burning** — creating a fire break

**Big Banana** — tourist attraction and information Center near Coffs Harbour, New South Wales

**Bloke** — man, guy

**Bluey** — common nickname for any male with red hair

**Boardwalk** — a timber walkway which can be built over rocks, sand or the forest floor

**Bushfire** — brush fire, wildfire, forest fire

**Caravan** — travel trailer

**Cuppa** — cup of tea

**Chook** — slang for chicken, also the nickname of the Bad Guy in this book

**Fireys** — Firemen - an affectionate term for volunteers who fight fires with the Rural Fire Service

**Grey Nomads** — retirees who travel around the country in RVs

**Hi-vis** — bright yellow or orange safety clothing, often fluorescent

**Ice** — crystal methamphetamine

**Jayco** — common brand of RVs

**LandCruiser** — 4WD Toyota LandCruiser, a popular choice to tow caravans in Australia

**Macca's** — McDonalds Fast Food restaurant

**Newsagent** — newsstand

**Nurofen, Nurofen Plus** — painkiller tablets

**Paddock** — a field

**Panadol** — similar to paracetamol & Tylenol - a common brand of painkiller in Australia

**RFS** — Rural Fire Service (a volunteer organization to fight the bushfires that rage in Australia every summer)

**Staghorn fern** — (also elk horn) a treetop fern that

has evolved to grow in the Australian rainforest; does not need soil

**Scrub turkey** — the Australian Brush-turkey. It has black body plumage, a bare red head and yellow throat wattle

**Tradie** — tradesman, anyone with a trade

**Ute** — utility truck or pickup

**Waeco fridge** — a common brand of portable fridge (car fridge)

**Water dragon** — a lizard that can stay submerged for up to an hour